'Just as long as you know that I've no intention of sharing a room with you.'

To her chagrin, Evan's stern mouth suddenly split in a grin, and Rowan's heart went racing like a wild animal let out of a trap. She couldn't prevent the wave of heat that ebbed through her blood at the thought of sharing a bed with the man. The one time they had made love it had been passionate and urgent, with little thought to linger and take things slowly, but what would a whole night in Evan's arms be like?

'We'll see,' he replied, stealing a brief amused glance at her indignant profile.

'What does that mean? I've already told you my decision and I'm sticking to it!'

'Protest any more and I might think you really want to spend the night with me.'

For several years **Maggie Cox** was a reluctant secretary who dreamed of becoming a published author. She can't remember a time when she didn't have her head in a book or wasn't busy filling exercise books with stories. When she was ten years old her favourite English teacher told her, 'If you don't become a writer I'll eat my hat!' But it was only after marrying the love of her life that she finally became convinced she might be able to achieve her dream. Now a self-confessed champion of dreamers everywhere, she urges everyone with a dream to go for it and never give up. Also a busy full-time mum, who tries constantly *not* to be so busy, in what she laughingly calls her spare time she loves to watch good drama or romantic movies, and eat chocolate!

Recent titles by the same author:

IN HER BOSS'S BED
A CONVENIENT MARRIAGE
THE MARRIAGE RENEWAL
A PASSIONATE PROTECTOR

A VERY PASSIONATE MAN

BY
MAGGIE COX

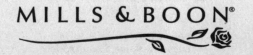

MILLS & BOON®

To Kate
For your faith and trust in me and for giving me this
wonderful chance. Mere thanks are not enough.

*First published in Great Britain 2004
Harlequin Mills & Boon Limited,
Eton House, 18-24 Paradise Road, Richmond, Surrey TW9 1SR*

© Maggie Cox 2004

ISBN 0 263 83758 0

*Set in Times Roman 10½ on 12¼ pt.
01-0704-46025*

*Printed and bound in Spain
by Litografía Rosés, S.A., Barcelona*

CHAPTER ONE

HE HAD no idea what drew him to the window just then. A sudden movement, perhaps, a glimpse of something white he'd caught out of the corner of his eye... If he'd wanted to dig deeper he would have said it was a feeling that drew him; a sense of something unexpected about to happen.

For some reason tension coiled in his stomach and made it hard to breathe. Evan put it down to the debilitating effects of burnout. Work had been the driving force in his life for too long and he was no longer able to kid himself that he could give himself up to its demands indefinitely—not unless he wanted an early death. That last bout of flu had damn near killed him. But what was he supposed to do now? He'd done what his doctor advised and taken a month off from his business to relax, walk on the beach, catch up on his reading...get his head on straight. As far as Evan was concerned, all were prospects that frankly held little appeal. Life for him equalled activity, and he'd always pushed his body to the maximum, whether in the gym or working ridiculous hours to promote his business. If only he had known that one day there would be a price to pay for such single-minded recklessness...

A sudden *frisson* of fear biting on his nerves, he clenched his jaw, green eyes narrowing at the sight that met his gaze through the window. Past the tumbledown, mildewed fence that needed mending, a woman, white straw hat, white cotton dress down to her ankles, stood amongst the crestfallen weeds of the neighbouring garden looking as if she'd somehow wandered on to the scene from the pages of *House and Garden*. Secateurs in one hand, a wicker basket in the other, it seemed to Evan that she glanced disconsolately at the sight before her, as if she might have taken on more than she could handle. Not that he could blame her. The old, run-down cottage had been empty for at least three years, maybe more. It had had a 'For Sale' sign stuck outside for maybe the same length of time. He should have noticed it had gone, but then he rarely came down to the coast these days—his sister, Beth, used the house more than he did. The evidence of her presence was everywhere, from the feminine paraphernalia dotted round the bathroom to the box of kids' toys stacked in the living-room behind a chintz curtain.

For some reason, the appearance of the woman in white irked him. He'd wanted peace. OK, so maybe he wasn't sure that he could handle it, but peace was what he'd had in mind as he'd made the long drive down from London yesterday. Now that peace had been infringed upon by the presence of an unexpected and unwanted neighbour. Rubbing at his forehead, Evan sensed the tension gathering there like a building thunderstorm. As long as she didn't bother him, everything would still go as he planned. Maybe she hadn't bought the house at all—maybe she was 'staging' it for a potential buyer? Wasn't that how they referred to it these days? But the face partially shielded by the big straw hat and the slender almost ethereal demeanour of the woman didn't immediately shout 'estate agent' to Evan. Angel, or ghost, but not estate agent.

Irked by such a ludicrous flight of fancy, he drew away from the window before she caught him staring. He glanced at the pile of hardbacks on the coffee-table, and walked moodily past them into the kitchen to make himself a drink. When he'd had his refreshment he'd take a long walk on the beach to help ease out the kinks in his tired, aching muscles. Perhaps his dour mood would improve after that.

Her train of thought suddenly lost, Rowan came to a standstill in the middle of the neglected little garden, staring down at the secateurs in her hand as if she couldn't quite fathom how they'd appeared there. She hated it when her thoughts were suddenly snatched away by this…this awful blankness. It was like wandering into a blinding mist after walking beneath a clear blue sky. Her fingers tightening round the smooth wooden handle of the pruning shears, she chewed down on her lip, willing herself to take charge, to be whole again—as she had been before Greg had died. But that girl had long gone, and the feeling of being apart from the rest of the world that had seized her that morning grew instead of lessened. Her heart galloped and her breath hitched, as if someone had sabotaged her oxygen supply. Instead of scrubby weeds, cheerful yellow dandelions and trailing bindweed, she saw her husband's face just before he'd left on his last assignment that hot August morning. Saw his plethora of camera gear hitched across his shoulder as she'd seen it many times before, such an integral part of him. The equipment was almost a metaphor for Greg's personal philosophy that, no matter how heavy your load, you just got on with life because after all, wasn't it a bonus that we were here at all? And, with that wicked boy-scout grin that could crowd her chest with warmth, he'd walked out of her life and into an oncoming car as he crossed the road to join the rest of his crew in the television-news van.

Rowan swallowed hard, willing herself to move before she took root where she was standing—just like one of the scrubby weeds she'd been so intent on removing. She'd never get anything done around here if she kept sabotaging her efforts like this. It wasn't just the garden that needed tending. The house also needed work to make it more habitable, even if she was destined to enjoy its comfort alone since Greg wasn't around any more to share it with her. The neglected little cottage, just a short walk away from the beach down a winding country lane, had captured their imaginations as soon as they'd seen it. They'd started making plans for its improvement the very moment they'd jumped out of the car to examine it. It would be their mission to return it to its former glory, they had vowed. In no time at all it would be the quintessential English country cottage, roses round the door and all. Hardly unique, but then they hadn't been planning on winning any prizes for originality—just making a home together.

After Greg had gone, it was the only place that Rowan could bear to be. Although it had been their dream, Greg had never actually lived in the house with her and so she wasn't going to be constantly reminded of his presence. Everything he'd owned she'd passed on to family, friends or charity shops and now, free of any physical reminders of the man who had been her husband, Rowan hoped to make a new life. 'Hoped' being the operative word. As yet she didn't seem to be getting very far.

The straw hat came bowling towards him as Evan lengthened his stride past her house. Another fierce gust of wind lifted it high above the broken wooden gate that leaned drunkenly on one rusty hinge and as he automatically reached out to grab it, he felt his sweater catch on one of the pointed wooden slats. Cursing softly, he unhooked himself, then raised his gaze to the slender figure in white drifting gracefully down the concrete path towards him. Evan's first glimpse of the woman's face without the protective shield of the hat told him that she was pretty, but unremarkable. As she drew nearer and he saw the tinge of pink shading her cheeks and the deep shyness reflected in soft, sherry-brown eyes he elevated his opinion to 'almost beautiful,' but his intention of keeping contact brief and strictly to the point didn't change. No sense in sending out the message that the aliens were friendly when Evan was feeling anything but.

'Thank you. Lucky for me you were passing just at the right moment.'

She flashed him a smile to accompany the soft, velvet voice that stroked over his nerve-endings, and a stab of heat caught him unawares. His black brows drew together in a scowl.

'Hardly the weather for straw hats, I would have thought.' As Evan handed over the recalcitrant hat he saw her smile quickly disappear to be replaced by a new, guarded look. Good. She'd got the message, then. Impatient to continue his walk, he turned away until her soft voice unexpectedly lured him back.

'Look around you.' Glancing up towards a cloudless blue sky, she was shielding her eyes from the almost too-bright glare of the sun. 'It's spring and soon it will be summer. Doesn't that make you want to acknowledge it in some way?'

Glancing at her long, pale arms in her white sleeveless dress, Evan angled his hard jaw disdainfully. 'I'd put on some more clothes if I were you. You'll catch your death out here in this cold wind.'

Ignoring possibly the most forbidding glower she'd ever seen, Rowan defiantly stuck out her hand towards him. 'I'm Rowan Hawkins. I moved in a few weeks ago and I'm very pleased to meet you. I was wondering when I'd meet my neighbours. Have you been away on holiday?'

'Look…what exactly do you want from me?'

Stunned, Rowan nervously licked her lips. 'I beg your pardon?'

'If you're expecting me to be all cosy and neighbourly then I'd like to set the record straight right now. I'm not the cosy or neighbourly type, Miss Hawkins, so save that annoyingly sunny smile of yours for someone else who might appreciate it. Do I make myself clear?'

Saying no more, Evan proceeded down the road, his broad shoulders squared against the fierce breeze that had gathered strength as they'd exchanged words, his hands dug deep into his jeans pockets. Watching him go, his long-legged stride carrying him purposefully away, Rowan felt her stomach sink like a stone. What an arrogant, unpleasant man! The hostility in those startling green eyes of his had genuinely shocked her. She wasn't used to eliciting such animosity in people and now, when she was feeling possibly at her most fragile, it was a double blow. That darkly handsome face of his certainly didn't invite a repeat introduction at a later date, and she would just have to console herself that she'd found out how unpleasant he was sooner rather than later. At least now she would be able to give him a wide berth when she saw him again. Trust her luck to live next door to a man who would make Genghis Khan seem like your average friendly neighbour!

Glancing down at the straw hat clenched tightly between her fingers, Rowan drew her softly shaped brows together in an anxious frown. Joking aside, how was she supposed to make a new start when even her closest neighbour didn't want to know her? With no heart to continue her pitiful attempt at gardening, she turned towards the house with a purposeful stride of her own—feeling not the slightest bit of remorse when she banged the front door noisily shut behind her.

The sound of Rowan Hawkins' broken gate swinging eerily back and forth on its solitary hinge damn near drove Evan to distraction that night. Unable to find sanctuary from his foul mood in sleep, he pushed to his feet, dragged back the filmy gauze curtain from the window that overlooked the moonlit garden next door, then glared at the offending gate as though his gaze alone could make it burst into flames.

Trouble was, it wasn't just the gate. Even the slightest thing seemed to irritate him out of all proportion these days. Anyway, you'd think her husband or boyfriend would fix the damn thing for her. She certainly didn't strike him as the type of woman who'd be happy to get her hands dirty doing anything practical like DIY. And who the hell dressed in white to do gardening? The woman clearly didn't have the sense that she was born with. Annoyed that his pretty neighbour was occupying more of his thoughts than she ought to be, Evan stalked into the kitchen to make a drink. When he discovered he was out of coffee his frustrated curse punctuated the air. Tunnelling his fingers through black hair, that if left long would have a distinct wave in it, he shut his eyes for a moment in a bid to calm down, but failed miserably as a stray memory of his ex-wife infiltrated its way stealthily into his mind. If Rebecca hadn't stung him for most of his wealth in their divorce settlement, he wouldn't have spent the past two years working himself into the ground to build up his fitness business again. Two gruelling years when he had sacrificed damn near everything—his home, his friends, his social life—to claw back most of what he had lost. It was testament to his blind single-mindedness that he had succeeded. The business was doing even better than ever. With over twenty fitness outlets all bearing the Evan Cameron name dotted round the country, he could afford to take things a little easier now. When he hadn't done any such thing, a three-week bout of influenza had made the decision to slow down for him. Slow down? Evan grimaced bitterly at the thought. Bring him to his knees, more like. In all his thirty-seven years he had never been so ill or so mentally and physically battle-scarred. To tell the truth, it had scared him rigid. How ironic that a man who promoted health and fitness had succumbed to illness all because of self-neglect.

Forcing himself to breathe more evenly, Evan opened a cupboard above the plain white counter in search of a malt drink. He should know better than to crave caffeine in the middle of the night, anyway. Five minutes later, his mood slightly improved and his drink made, he sought out the big, squashy sofa in the comfortably furnished living-room then reached for the remote and switched on the TV. As he strove to concentrate on yet another rerun of *The African Queen* unfolding before him, he tried to blot out the sound of Rowan Hawkins' rickety gate creaking noisily back and forth.

Rowan was attempting to replace the rusty hinges on the gate. Dressed in jeans and a skinny-rib red sweater, her glossy brown hair scooped back into a pony-tail, she tried in vain to unscrew the tightly embedded steel screw in the one remaining hinge. Trouble was, her hands were freezing. The sun was shining but the icy wind cut like a razor and she could barely get enough leverage on the screwdriver to turn the thing at all. 'Damn!'

Could anyone blame her if she felt like sitting there and crying like a baby? First she'd discovered she'd acquired a Neanderthal for a neighbour, and second she'd learned that 'do it yourself' was definitely not her natural province. She would just have to spend some of the small legacy Greg had left her after paying for the house on funding some urgently needed jobs that needed doing round the place. Like this gate. It should have been so simple. It *looked* simple, Rowan reflected, as her brow knit in frustration. But right now splitting the atom might be simpler.

'Having trouble?'

Rowan glanced up in shock at the deep, masculine voice and heat rushed into her body as if she'd been dropped into a vat of hot water. Frosty eyes the colour of green ice stared back at her with disconcerting directness. Despite a helpless stirring of rage swirling deep in her belly, she couldn't help but be compelled to study the tough male visage. He was without a doubt commandingly masculine yet at the same time beautiful, and Rowan was even more disturbed by him than she had been on their first encounter—when hc'd grudgingly halted the escape of her wayward straw hat. But, all the same, she'd be damned if she would give him the satisfaction of thinking she was some kind of helpless little woman who didn't know what she was doing.

'I'm fine, thank you.'

Laying down the screwdriver, she rubbed her hands briskly together to get the circulation flowing back into her cramped fingers, deliberately keeping her expression carefully blank.

'That damn gate of yours kept me awake all night with its creaking.' Folding his arms across a chest that was disconcertingly wide, with muscles like steel beneath his black sweater if the strongly corded sinews in his forearms were anything to go by, Rowan's hostile neighbour presented her with yet another forbidding scowl.

'Why do you think I'm trying to fix it? It kept me awake too.' That and another awful nightmare about Greg walking out in front of that car...

'So you know what you're doing, then?'

She thought she saw just a hint of a smile touch those austere-looking lips of his, but then told herself she must be mistaken. Something told her that smiles from this man would be as unlikely as honeysuckle growing in the Arctic. Anyhow, she was too busy being incensed by that superior, condescending tone of his to care one way or the other.

'Frankly, Mr Whatever-Your-Name-Is, it's none of your business. Now, I'd really appreciate it if you'd just leave me alone and let me get on with it.'

'Evan Cameron.'

'What?' Rowan blinked up at him.

'My name. It's Evan Cameron.' *But don't get your hopes up. Just because I've told you my name it doesn't mean we're going to be friends.* She heard the words echo through her head even though he hadn't actually voiced them.

'Fine. Good. I'll know who you are if anyone knocks on my door by mistake, then.' Her fingers curled around the screwdriver again and determinedly she trained all her concentration on trying to undo the obstinate screw.

'Give it to me.'

'What?'

The screwdriver was deftly removed from between her freezing-cold fingers before she even knew what was happening. Shocked by the contact of his larger, rougher hand brushing against hers, Rowan stood up to her full five feet five inches and glared at the black-haired whipcord-lean specimen of forbidding male towering over her.

'Why don't you get inside in the warm and I'll see to this?'

If he'd meant to sound solicitous of her welfare all of a sudden, Rowan itched to tell him that he'd failed. Her creaking gate had annoyed him, that was all, and he was anxious to get it fixed so he wouldn't have to endure another sleepless night because of it. Another woman might be grateful he was going to fix it at all and save her a job, but not Rowan. As far as she was concerned, if someone couldn't offer help with a good heart then it wasn't really help at all. She'd rather blunder on under her own steam and make a pig's ear of the job than allow some hostile male with an overstated sense of his own machismo to take charge.

'I didn't ask for your help and neither do I require it, Mr Cameron. I'm sure you have better things to do than stand out here in the cold and fix my annoying gate on a Sunday morning.'

Holding out her hand, Rowan tried to ignore the thundering of her heart as her own soft brown eyes duelled with frosty green. 'I'd like my screwdriver back, please.'

'You got a man about the house, *Ms* Hawkins?'

'That's none of your business. And before you say anything else, don't you dare stand there and condescend to treat me like some vacuous little female who doesn't know one end of a power tool from another, because I—'

'Do you?' Evan's lips twitched into a smile before he could help it.

Her shoulders stiffening in resentment, Rowan glared in disbelief. 'Do I what?'

'Know one end of a power tool from another?'

'This is ridiculous! Give me my screwdriver and just go. Please go!'

'Please yourself.' Shrugging those broad shoulders of his as if he really didn't give a damn, Evan returned the tool to her outstretched hand. He turned to walk away, then stopped and glanced back for a few disturbing seconds, his cool gaze sizing Rowan up as if he definitely found her wanting in the physical department. 'Funny how the phrase ''cutting off your nose to spite your face'' springs to mind. Fix that gate, Ms Hawkins, or I'll be knocking on your door in the middle of the night so that you can share my night-time torment.'

And with that he walked away, as if he were some arrogant lord of the manor and she a mere peasant trespassing on his land. Giving vent to her fury, Rowan jammed the screwdriver back into the screw and nearly howled in pain when it slipped and almost took the skin off her thumb.

Two hours later, her belly grumbling for lunch and her body stiff with cold, Rowan got up off her knees and had to admit defeat. Two hours…two hours, for God's sake! And that damn hinge still wouldn't budge. As she hurried back up the path towards the house, she glanced surreptitiously at her neighbour's windows. Satisfied that she wasn't being observed, she rushed inside and carefully shut the door behind her. Ten minutes later, phone directory in one hand and a steaming mug of hot chocolate in the other to warm her, Rowan sat herself down at the circular pine kitchen table with the telephone to see if she could locate a nearby odd-job man. She was still seething from Evan Cameron's parting remark— 'night-time torment' indeed! She was just about to pick up the phone to punch out a number when the melodic sound of the doorbell trilled ominously through the house.

'You've got guts, I'll give you that.'

'Meaning?'

Bristling at the humour in Evan Cameron's previously glacial green eyes as his awesome physique dominated her doorway, Rowan didn't know how she resisted the urge to slap that smirk clean off his wretchedly handsome face.

'For two hours now I've watched you struggle with that hinge in the cold and wind, and, whatever I think of your misguided stubbornness to prove a point, I've got to respect the fact that you didn't give up trying. Let me put you out of your misery and mend the gate for you, then I promise I won't bother you again.'

CHAPTER TWO

'WHAT does it take to get through that thick skull of yours?' Rowan heard herself demand. 'I don't want you to fix my gate. If I can't fix it myself then I'd rather any other man in the world fixed it than you!'

The woman was even more stubborn than he'd thought. Evan knew he was mostly to blame for her current animosity towards him, but still he'd gone to her house with the best of intentions, and was it his fault if she refused to see that it made utter sense for him to fix her broken gate? She'd said she'd rather 'any other man in the world' fix it than him. Perhaps there wasn't a husband or boyfriend around, then? There must be a good reason she was trying to repair the damn thing herself.

His green eyes narrowed with reluctant interest. In her floaty white dress of yesterday Rowan Hawkins had looked small and unbelievably slender. Today, in tight black jeans and a figure-hugging red sweater, Evan could see she had curves in plenty. His gaze was momentarily distracted by the angry rise and fall of her eye-catching breasts beneath her sweater and he cursed the inevitable reaction low in his groin. Despite his purely male response she really wasn't his type at all. He liked his women taller and on the willowy side. He especially wasn't attracted to women with that lost look in their pretty brown eyes, or women who thought it was an infringement of their human rights if a man so much as held a door open for them—never mind offered to mend broken gates.

'Fine.'

Only it wasn't fine. Not really. There was still the little matter of the creaking gate potentially keeping him awake for a second night in a row. The wind coming in off the sea was still fierce, and even now the damn thing was squeaking for all it was worth. If it carried on any longer he'd be fit to be tied.

'Perhaps you could get your husband to fix it, then?'

Evan knew by the sudden shadows that crept into her eyes that he'd said the wrong thing. He'd deliberately baited her just for the hell of it. Oh, why hadn't he just left well enough alone and walked away? He was the one who'd told her he wasn't the neighbourly sort and now he was annoying himself with his dogged persistence in trying to win a response from her.

'I don't have a husband.'

'Not the end of the world.' Shrugging, Evan dug his hands into his jeans pockets, wondering how he could tactfully withdraw from the pain that was all too evident in her soft brown gaze. 'You're probably better off without one. I can't say the married state is one I'd recommend.'

'Really? Your cold cynicism can't win you many friends, Mr Cameron. For your information, my husband was killed in a road accident. I loved him with all my heart and miss him like you can't begin to imagine, so how do you figure that I'm better off without him?'

Her voice breaking on a sob, Rowan retreated, stricken, behind the solid wooden door with its peeling white paint and the sound of it slamming reverberated through Evan's skull like cannon fire. For a long moment he simply didn't move. Of all the crass, tactless, supremely stupid things that had ever come out of his mouth, his last comment to Rowan was probably the worst. Now not only did he loathe his own apparent inability to be even the smallest bit sensitive to a woman who was clearly in pain, but he also detested the unhappy knack he'd acquired in the past two years of distancing himself emotionally from the rest of the human race. Since Rebecca had done her worst it had been Evan's safety valve, but now he despised himself for allowing it to become a habit.

He considered knocking on Rowan's door again to apologise, but realised that under the circumstances she'd probably just tell him to go to hell. Too late, he was there already... He clicked his tongue and backtracked down the path to stare down at the offending gate with a rueful shake of his head.

An hour later he had it mended, new hinges and all. The curtain at one of Rowan's front windows twitched slightly as Evan stood up, but he deliberately glanced away, stretching his arms high above his head to ease out the cramp in his muscles before gathering up his tools. He had no intention of waiting around for acknowledgement of what he'd done— not that he expected it. Instead, closing the gate smartly behind him with a satisfying click, he strode back down the path to his own house and headed straight for the television remote in the living-room. He'd drown out the painful self-recrimination tumbling around in his head with the athletics meet that the BBC were broadcasting and hopefully forget about everything else but the pursuit of athletic excellence and competing with the best.

Her fingers embedded in dough, Rowan paused in her energetic kneading to stare out the window at her poor, bedraggled garden. The grass was almost bald in places and in others it grew wild and free, vying with the weeds for precedence. She'd have to lay some new turf if she wanted a lawn, but first she needed to tackle those weeds and cut the wild grass down to a more manageable length. On a positive note, there was plenty to delight the eye as well. Little clumps of sunny primula and bunches of bright yellow daffodils swayed in the breeze, and there were even a few dainty bluebells stating their presence amongst the green.

What had possessed Evan Cameron to fix her creaking gate after everything she'd said? For the umpteenth time that afternoon, Rowan's thoughts gravitated back to him. Had he felt guilty when she'd told him that her husband was dead? No. The man simply didn't seem capable of such a human emotion. Clearly he just hadn't been able to endure another night's broken sleep, that was all. He'd simply been looking after his own interests when he'd decided to assume the role of odd-job man. Well,

OK…as long as he didn't expect her to be grateful. From now on she really would give him a wide berth and she certainly wouldn't waste another one of her 'annoyingly sunny' smiles on him again, even if he begged her. Which, of course, he wouldn't. A man who looked like Evan Cameron would never have to beg a woman for anything—that was if they were prepared to overlook the unrelenting chill in those fascinating green eyes of his. What was his story, she wondered. What had put the strain around that austere mouth? The tiny grooves in that otherwise smooth, almost olive skin of his? And why would a man like him want to bury himself in the depths of the countryside like some kind of hermit?

'Think about something else, why don't you?' Incensed with herself for spending too much time dwelling on the man, Rowan pounded the innocent dough with more force than was strictly necessary. But there was great satisfaction in having an unexpected outlet for the rage that had been boiling inside her since Evan Cameron's offensive remarks that morning. If the man were hanging off the edge of a cliff she wouldn't raise one finger to help him. No. She'd just smile sweetly and wave goodbye. As far as Rowan was concerned, he could plummet into oblivion and good riddance!

Half an hour later, a steak and kidney pie simmering in the oven and the washing-up done and put away, Rowan returned to her living-room to sort through some old photographs. She'd been putting off the task since she moved into the cottage a month ago, but now there was no reason—except maybe fear—for her not doing it. She'd already decided there were too many pictures for her to keep, and anyway, why did she want reminders of what Greg had looked like? His beloved features were imprinted on her heart for always. Looking at photographs of happier times would only bring her pain, and it wasn't as if she had children to keep them for. A pulse throbbed in her temple at the thought.

Settling the two old-fashioned biscuit tins side by side on the dark wood table, Rowan carefully prised off the lid of one of them, then, taking a deep, shuddering breath to steel herself, picked up a handful of photographs and studied them. Now, there was a man who had known how to smile. First picture she'd handled and there was Greg, grinning cheerfully into her camera, for once happy to be in front of the lens instead of behind it. It had been taken on a stolen day out at the seaside, and the pair of them had behaved like a couple of carefree children. Eating huge ice creams as they strolled along the promenade, having fun at the small fairground, then eating fish and chips for their tea as they sat on the sand and watched the tide come in, they'd honestly believed they had a wonderful future in prospect.

Her throat tightening with a now familiar ache, Rowan stroked the glossy picture, her heart swelling with love and pride at the man she had loved and lost. Greg had had a nice face. Not handsome or good-looking, but a *good* face that people had been instantly drawn to. His sunny, benevolent nature hadn't disappointed either. At his funeral there had been friends and colleagues in plenty along with family to mourn his untimely passing.

Rowan's mind drifted along on a sea of remembrance. She could hardly believe that almost seven months had gone by since the accident. After spending the first three months after Greg's death in a kind of numbed existence, where she'd got up, washed, dressed, ate breakfast and gone to work, it had slowly dawned on her that she should sell the house in Battersea. Instead, she would take up residence in their 'nest egg'—the dream cottage that they had bought in wild and beautiful Pembrokeshire. All of a sudden she had known a desperate desire to escape the noisy, gridlocked city and take refuge in some peace and quiet.

Now that she was here, she couldn't help wondering if she had bitten off more than she could chew. So much needed to be done, and Rowan was a city girl who had lived in London all her life. Working as a production assistant for a busy, up-and-coming television company, she hadn't had time to develop an interest in 'do it yourself' and neither, bless him, had Greg. He had either been away for long periods on assignments all over the world or at the studio doing important research for his next job. Sighing as she glanced around at the dilapidated shelves that needed painting and repositioning, the wooden floor that needed sanding down and varnishing before she could adorn it with the beautiful rugs Greg had brought back from his travels, Rowan knew she would seriously have to get down to learning how to do some of these jobs herself. If she was going to take a whole year out of work as she'd planned, then she couldn't afford to pay workmen to do all the jobs that needed doing round the house to make it habitable.

Already she felt that she'd failed in some way because Evan Cameron had had to come to her rescue and fix her damn creaky gate. Well, she'd show him! That was the last time he was going to treat her like some dull-witted, pathetic female who didn't have a clue how to do anything more complicated than paint her toenails! Suddenly realising that sorting through her photographs wasn't the task that most needed doing after all, Rowan dropped the pictures back into their tin and jammed the lid down hard. As the delicious aroma of cooking meat pie started to pervade the house, she jumped up and disappeared into her bedroom to rummage through her bookshelves for the two second-hand books she had purchased a week ago on home decorating and 'Do It Yourself for the Enthusiastic Beginner'.

His black hair sleek from his shower and a striped bath towel secured around his toned-hard middle, Evan took his time crossing the room to get to the ringing telephone. Only two people—as far as he was aware—knew his whereabouts. Right now, the mood he was in, he didn't relish speaking to either of them.

'Yes?' He deliberately didn't announce his name or number, and he most definitely didn't put out a vibe that came anywhere close to friendly.

'Evan, is that you?' rejoined a familiar female voice.

'Beth,' he sighed, and wondered how soon he could bring the call to an end without being rude. Five years younger than her big brother, his sister still acted like a mother hen around him. 'How are the kids?'

'Luke and Alex are fine. It's not them I'm concerned about, as well you know.'

'And from that do I deduce that *I'm* the focus of all your loving concern?'

'It's not a joke, Evan. A couple of months ago you nearly died of the flu! It's only natural that I want to keep in touch to make sure everything's all right. Are you eating OK? I know you're big on all that nutritional stuff for fitness, but are you getting enough fresh fruit and veg? You know there's that handy little greengrocers in the village, don't you? Their stuff is pretty good, and they even stock things like nuts and seeds.'

'Thanks for the tip.'

'Don't be sarcastic.'

'I'm not.' Wearily sinking down into a nearby armchair, Evan leaned back against the flattened cushions and stared blankly at the hand that he'd rested against his thigh. It was shaking. Ever so slightly, but shaking just the same. He hadn't told Beth that he'd had the shakes for several months now. They had started even before he'd been struck down with flu. A common symptom of severe stress, his doctor had explained. Flexing his fingers, Evan tried to convince himself he wasn't concerned. The doctor had advised rest and that was what he was doing. No lifting weights, no strenuous exercise and definitely no jogging. Swimming and walking were, however, recommended. Thank God for that or else he'd go completely crazy.

'Evan?' Shrill with worry, Beth's voice jerked him back to the present.

'It's OK. I'm still here.'

'You don't sound very happy, that's all.'

'Don't read too much into it. Nobody's loved me yet for my great sense of humour.'

'I feel like I ought to come down for a visit, make sure you're looking after yourself. Maybe I could stay for a couple of days without the kids? I could ask Paul's mum to have them.'

Evan sat up straight. 'No offence, Beth, but I really don't want any visitors—nor do I need looking after. All I need is some time to get my head together. I'll maybe ring you in a few days and let you know how I'm doing, OK?' It was an effort to keep the strain out of his voice but he hoped he managed it. The last thing he needed right now was for his baby sister to descend on him and take it upon herself to look after him. Besides, he wasn't feeling up to conversation with anyone. Not yet. His last attempt with Rowan Hawkins next door had failed miserably and he was in no hurry to repeat the experience any time soon.

'Well, if you're sure you're all right?'

'I'm fine, Beth. Really.'

'Well, you know where I am if you need me. By the way, I hope you've told them at work that you're not to be disturbed?'

Evan recalled his last conversation with Mike, his

second in command. 'Don't hesitate to call me if you're unsure about something or if anything important comes up.' Mike had given him a cursory nod in reply, which told Evan that the man was ever so slightly offended that Evan clearly didn't trust him enough to take charge. Which wasn't true at all. It was just that Evan couldn't help but feel redundant when he wasn't allowed to be in control. If his three-week battle with flu hadn't left him with chronic fatigue and muscle ache, he'd probably be back at work now—even against doctor's orders.

'Mike won't call me unless he really has to.' He pushed to his feet, impatient to bring the call to an end.

'I suppose I'll just have to trust that you won't do anything foolish, then, like working out or undertaking a twenty-mile hike or something stupid like that.'

'No chance.' The thought that he couldn't physically do either of those things right now was like a spear through his heart. It emasculated him somehow…made him feel less like a man, when previously he'd been so awesomely fit. Suddenly shivering with the cold, Evan was anxious for Beth to be gone so he could dress.

'See you, then.'

'Bye, sis. Give the boys a hug for me.'

Rowan knew it was a stupid thing to do but, knowing she was driving into town for groceries and hardware supplies, she couldn't help but believe it was rude not to ask her neighbour if he needed anything. She hadn't seen him around for a few days, but his car—

a brand-spanking-new Land Rover—was still parked outside. In her hands she carried a peace offering: a plastic container filled with newly baked fruit scones. Well, she reasoned, she couldn't eat them all herself, could she? And everyone knew that scones didn't freeze well.

Lifting the heavy brass knocker, Rowan rapped smartly on his door before she lost her nerve, all the while her heartbeat thudding like the knell of doom inside her chest. Hearing footsteps approach, she steeled herself as Evan opened the door. There was a startled shift in his unsettling green eyes as he silently regarded her and Rowan stood mesmerised, unable to think of even one thing to say. Dressed in faded blue jeans with a rip in one knee and a black T-shirt, Evan Cameron's hard, fit body elevated the ordinary, everyday clothing to something else entirely…something almost illicit, leaning heavily towards the dangerously sexual. For long, worrying seconds Rowan was completely transfixed by the sight of those bulging, taut biceps, with their straining sinews that his scant clothing drew immediate attention to. Something in the pit of her stomach sizzled like coals on a barbecue and sucked all the moisture from her mouth.

'I—I thought you might like some of these.' She pressed the plastic container into his hands, then quickly retreated. 'Scones. I just made them.'

Evan silently contemplated the box he'd unwittingly accepted, then raised his gaze to pin Rowan to the spot. Her cheeks were arrestingly rosy and her pretty brown eyes shy and uncertain. For the life of him Evan didn't have a clue why she would want to present him with the results of her baking—not after their last encounter.

'Thanks.'

Was that all he was going to say? Rowan knew a moment of sheer blind panic. What on earth had possessed her to approach the man again? It should have been obvious to a blind woman that he clearly didn't want anything to do with her.

'You're welcome.' Her slim shoulders shrugged beneath her green waxed jacket. 'I'm going into town to do some shopping. I wondered if you needed anything?'

'I only repaired your gate, Ms Hawkins—not rescued you from drowning.'

She felt heat rush to her cheeks in a hot flood. He was smiling, damn him! Looking at her like the epitome of the Big Bad Wolf, with his slightly dishevelled black hair and even blacker brows. No man had ever gazed upon her in such a...*licentious* manner before. What on earth was she supposed to do now?

'I'm quite aware of that. I know you're not interested in being ''neighbourly,'' as you put it, but I hadn't seen you around for a couple of days and thought you might be unwell or something. In which case you might—you might need me to...' Her words dwindled to silence as Evan continued to study her as if she was suddenly the most interesting woman on the planet. Helplessly, her gaze gravitated back to his biceps. Oh, why couldn't the man take pity and go and put on a sweater?

'There's nothing I need right now.' His voice was

almost akin to a honeyed growl and Rowan nearly tripped over her own feet in her haste to engineer some distance between them. 'But thanks for thinking of me…and for these.' He held up the box and gave it a little shake.

'Anyway.' Hitching the strap of her black leather bag more securely onto her shoulder, Rowan pushed back a mutinous strand of hair that had flicked across her face. 'I'd better go. Lots to do.'

'Don't let me keep you,' Evan said behind her as she scurried back down the path. Was it her fevered imagination or had he laced the innocent-sounding comment with a taunt?

Inside, Evan leant back against the door and prised the lid off the plastic box. The mouthwatering aroma of still-warm baking drifted tantalisingly beneath his nose.

'Hmm.' Smiling to himself, he closed the lid. 'You do know how to tempt a man, pretty little Rowan. I wonder what other delights you're capable of surprising a man with…apart from your cooking, that is?'

Alarmed to find himself pleasantly aroused, Evan strode irritably into the kitchen, promising himself that from now on he'd give the arresting little widow zero encouragement when it came to getting over-friendly. He didn't want anyone invading his self-imposed isolation, and right now he had no use for a woman who was nursing a hurt he couldn't begin to imagine how to alleviate. But as he flipped open the plastic container and helped himself to a warm, melting scone, Evan's fertile imagination made a liar of that last statement. Unbidden, the thought of Rowan warming his bed and helping to tangle his sheets with that sweet, curvy body of hers stole into his mind like forbidden fruit…all the more exciting because under the circumstances the very idea was totally outrageous.

CHAPTER THREE

HER shopping done, Rowan didn't rush to get back home. Instead she found a welcoming little bistro tucked away in a cobblestoned side-street and treated herself to fresh salmon cakes with a lemon butter sauce and a glass of wine. Satisfied after her meal, she paid her bill and stepped out into the surprisingly mild spring evening. By the time she got into her car and drove out of the town, back onto the country roads, she was feeling pleasantly tired and looking forward to a peaceful evening curled up on the couch with her soft cashmere throw and a book. In the boot of her car were her grocery shopping and two big carrier-bags full of handy items for sprucing up the cottage. The next day she planned to get cracking on her home improvements, telling herself she'd start by removing all the pine shelves in the living-room and giving them a cheerful coat of paint.

When she pulled up in front of the cottage, it was all she could do to unlock the boot and unload her shopping, she was so tired. But as she busied herself standing the bags side by side on the road, the sound of footsteps approaching made her spin round in alarm. Attired in dark jeans and a black polo-necked sweater, Evan Cameron drew up beside Rowan and blew into his hands. The ensuing steam from his breath curled up into the night. The scent of the sea was all around him and he had clearly been walking on the beach. Beads of perspiration stood out on his lightly grooved brow but his imperious green gaze was decidedly cool when Rowan automatically smiled her surprise.

'Oh. It's you. It's a lovely evening for a walk, isn't it?'

His gaze flicked over her figure in her waxed jacket and long black skirt and boots. Her soft brown hair was loose, blowing around her face in the breeze, her cheeks pink like two rosy apples. There was something wholesome about her that pricked at Evan's conscience, something that made his frustration with himself and the current limitations of his body hard to bear. He'd undertaken a simple half-hour walk to the beach and back and his heart was racing as if he'd run a marathon. His irritation tightened like a noose around his neck as he studied Rowan.

'What are you trying to do, Ms Hawkins? Change my mind about you? I told you I wasn't interested in being neighbourly yet you seem to persist in the idea that you can somehow win me over. First it's with your baking—and next?' His insolent stare left Rowan in no doubt as to his meaning. Her body went hot and cold all at once. If she could have disappeared inside her coat right then and hidden, she would have.

'I don't know what you're talking about, Mr Cameron. Do you think I'm so desperate I would do anything to cultivate a friendship with you? I may be a widow but I'd rather spend fifty years locked up in a windowless cell than spend any more time than I could help in your hateful company!'

He laughed, and the cold, harsh sound splintered through the air like ice cracking on a frozen lake. Rowan winced.

'Good.' Evan nodded his dark head as if he had her measure. 'It's good to know you're not as meek as you appear. Believe me, Rowan, you really would be better off being locked up in a windowless cell than spending time in my company. If you don't believe me, try having a conversation about it with my ex-wife. She'll put you right.'

Stunned by his bitter response, Rowan felt her own reply stall in her throat. Her smile long gone, her liquid brown eyes were round with hurt as they regarded him.

'I'm sorry if you feel I've been a nuisance. Please be assured I won't be bothering you again. Now, if you'll excuse me, I have to get my shopping inside.'

She heard him curse beneath his breath, but she couldn't tell if it was directed at her or at himself. Either way, he didn't hang around for her to find out. When Rowan straightened from lifting her bags, he was already opening the gate to his own cottage and sprinting up the path. Seconds later the sound of his door slamming echoed through the night like a retort from a rifle.

Rowan couldn't get to sleep. Shaky and angry since Evan's verbal attack on her attempt at friendliness earlier, she now lay awake with the lamp turned on, her book opened unread by her side and her eyes gritty with fatigue because sleep eluded her.

What was it about her that the man disliked so much? He'd mentioned an ex-wife. Was it Rowan's misfortune to remind him of her in some way? Had their parting been so acrimonious that he still harboured a grudge against the woman?

Her thoughts ran on and on, finding no resolution from her endless speculation about the cold, autocratic man who lived next door—how could it, when her day had been completely spoiled by her confrontation with him? Drawing her knees up to her chest, she folded her arms around them with a sigh. If only Greg were here. He'd know just what to say to comfort her. He'd probably pull her head down onto his chest, stroke her hair and tell her she shouldn't waste another moment's anxiety on Evan Cameron because clearly the man was an ignorant peasant and it was his loss if he didn't want to be neighbourly. He'd follow up this statement with some witty observation about the man's character that would make Rowan laugh. Oh, how she missed Greg's laughter. He'd always had a natural ability to see the brighter side of life even when things appeared dire. She had envied him that. She had always been the serious one, the one urging caution, when Greg merely threw caution to the wind and laughed in its face. He should be here with her now, talking over the improvements they were going to make on the house together. Instead…instead…

Rowan pushed off the bed and swept her hand through her hair, wishing she could sweep away the dark thoughts racing through her mind as easily. Pacing up and down across the thick patterned carpet that she would replace just as soon as she could afford to, she swallowed down the painful ache in her throat and refused to let the tears that were threatening come. OK, so she was a widow—she wasn't the first woman in the world who had suffered the loss of a husband and, dear God, she wouldn't be the last. If all those other women could survive the hurt and desolation, then so could Rowan. She'd come this far without falling to pieces, hadn't she? And what exactly had Evan Cameron meant when he'd said it was good she wasn't as meek as she appeared? The mere thought of the man made her feel about as meek as a rampaging rhinoceros! She had a good mind to knock on his door right now and verbally rip his arrogant head off—then he might really discover what 'night-time torment' meant!

But, of course, she would do no such thing. He'd probably coolly brush her off with that disdainful look that came so naturally, or, worse, phone the police and tell them he had a mad woman living next door and could they please come and lock her up in a cell for the night so he could get some sleep? Frustration and anger eating her up, Rowan grabbed her robe and headed straight for the kitchen. Switching on the lights, then opening the fridge, she carefully extracted the fruit pie she'd made earlier when she'd baked her batch of scones. Carrying it to the small pine table set in an alcove, she cut herself a generous wedge and bit into it with tears streaming hotly from her eyes and sliding helplessly into her mouth.

*   *   *

Staring at the two small but stinging cuts he'd in-advertently made at the edge of his jaw with his ra-zor, Evan winced as he pressed his fingers to them to momentarily staunch the thick ooze of blood. He hadn't had the shakes this morning, thank God, but his concentration was shot to hell anyway. He'd been evil to the pretty little widow next door and he wasn't proud of the fact. If Beth had borne witness to his boorishness she would probably have been ashamed to call herself his sister. Damn it, he was ashamed of his outlandish behaviour himself! Venting his spleen on Rowan just because he wasn't the man he'd used to be was unforgivable. Her hurt brown eyes had stared back at him as if he were a careless motorist who'd just run over her puppy.

Meeting his sombre reflection in the bathroom mirror, Evan let loose a ripe curse. With the cuts on his jaw oozing blood and his black brows drawn to-gether giving him a decidedly forbidding expression, all he needed was a black eye-patch and some dark stubble round his chin and he'd resemble Blackbeard the Pirate. If he were in Rowan's shoes, he'd give himself a very wide berth indeed.

But just the same, he wasn't going to apologise. Hadn't Evan already told her in more ways than one that he wasn't going to encourage her acquaintance? Was the woman a glutton for punishment, giving him those shy, girlish smiles of hers that would likely melt a heart of stone? Except his heart, of course. As he moved back into his bedroom to raid his wardrobe for clothes, he mused that it wasn't his fault she was a widow and she was lonely. Any other man would probably want to take advantage of such a situation, but Evan knew better than to buy a whole load of trouble he could very well live without. It had taken two gruelling, hardworking years to get Rebecca out of his system and he was in no hurry to get involved with another woman—no matter how attractive or appealing.

Yanking on his jeans, then pulling another black sweater down over his head, Evan made his way out to the kitchen in search of some breakfast. For some inexplicable reason he was extraordinarily hungry this morning, and that surprised him. His previously healthy appetite had dwindled to a quarter of what he normally ate since he'd had that damned flu. Opening the fridge, he withdrew a box of eggs, a packet of bacon and a punnet of tomatoes that he'd bought the previous weekend but which were still within their sell-by date. Then, rifling through overhead cupboards, he retrieved a family-sized frying-pan and set it with down with satisfaction on the cooker.

The smell of paint had given Rowan a headache. To counteract the effect, she'd carried the three pine shelves outside and propped them up against the faded wrought-iron bench that sat in the front garden. With her hair in a loose topknot, and suitably attired in old blue corduroys and a chunky-knit sweater of Greg's that she couldn't bring herself to give away, Rowan momentarily savoured the fresh country breeze that rustled by before carefully applying another coat of bright lilac paint to one of the shelves.

Accidentally her gaze fell on Evan's smart blue Land Rover, parked outside the pretty whitewashed cottage where he lived, and she quickly withdrew it back to her painting before he spied her looking. Unless he'd walked down to the beach or the village he must still be in the house, she surmised. In which case, the lower the profile she kept—the better. The last thing in the world she needed right now was a repeat performance of last night's horrible confrontation.

She'd been painting for almost an hour when she heard the door of the neighbouring cottage slam. As she automatically glanced across, Rowan's surprised, slightly panicked gaze locked with Evan's. When she looked away again, her pulse skittering like a nervous colt, she told herself to pay the man no attention and get back to what she was doing without giving him a second thought. Easier said than done when his footsteps seemed intent on heading her way…

'I'll come straight to the point.'

Rowan's gaze travelled from his black-booted feet all the way up those long, straight legs of his in dark blue denim, past the wide shoulders in his black sweater, finally arriving at the ominously serious expression currently fixed on his face. For the first time it wasn't his remarkable green eyes that instantly demanded her attention but the sexy little dimple in the centre of his well-defined jaw instead. Instantly, she rebuked herself for noticing such a thing.

'You'll come straight to the point about what?' she asked, affecting indifference. When he didn't reply immediately, she placed her dripping paintbrush carefully across the paint tin and waited for him to continue. He shifted from one lean hip to the other. 'I owe you an apology.'

'You do?' One slender brown eyebrow shot skywards and she couldn't help the sarcasm that dripped into her tone. In a million years if someone had told her that the arrogant Evan Cameron would march up her path and tell her he owed her an apology she would have called them deluded.

'It's not your fault that I prefer my own company most of the time.'

'This is an apology?' Rocking back on her heels, Rowan stoically fought back the urge to grin. The man looked so uncomfortable it was painful. Clearly he didn't find it easy to say those two relatively simple words 'I'm sorry'. She suddenly felt desperately sad for his friends.

Spearing his fingers through the thick mane of dark hair that touched his collar, Evan shook his head. 'You're going to milk this for all its worth aren't you?' His voice was cold.

Deciding to put the poor man out of his misery, Rowan wiped her hands down her thighs in the corduroy trousers then rose carefully to her feet.

'Forget it. I don't need you to apologise. I understand perfectly why you behave the way you do. You value your privacy above all else. You wanted to be alone, and because my cottage has been empty for so long you naturally assumed it would stay empty. My presence has taken you by surprise. You don't really want me here. I can understand that too. I probably moved here for the same reasons—to be alone, to hear myself think. But unlike you, Mr

Cameron, however much I like my own company I don't see any harm in passing the time of day with my fellow human beings. Sometimes it has positive benefits. Just a smile from another person can totally lift my mood. I'm not asking you to move in with me or be my mentor—I didn't even ask you to mend my broken gate. I'm simply exchanging hello's or good morning's, nice, normal greetings that don't require anything other than a smile or a similar greeting in return. Nothing too challenging in that, wouldn't you agree?'

Her little speech took him aback, and not just because there was a lot of truth in it. It was the passion in that usually soft, velvet voice that caught Evan by surprise. Suddenly he saw her in a different light. Clearly when this woman loved she did it wholeheartedly and without reservation. For some reason Evan experienced a shaft of pure envy of the man Rowan Hawkins had loved and lost. His gaze swept across her face, saw the rebellious glint reflected in those pretty brown eyes with their curling dark lashes, the man's sweater at least three sizes too big that swamped her slender frame and knew without doubt it had belonged to her husband. When she was alone in her bed at night, did she ache for him still?

Rowan wondered at the sudden surge of heat that shaded Evan's lean, hard jaw. Had she gone too far in speaking her mind the way she had? Had she made things worse instead of better? Expelling an impatient breath, she stared down forlornly at the tin of paint. A couple of drips from the brush had splashed onto the concrete path, creating two lilac splotches that resembled buttons. Raising her eyes to Evan's, she folded her arms defensively across her chest.

'If you've nothing else to say then I really must get on. I wanted to get these shelves done before this afternoon because the forecast said rain.'

'I'm sorry I was rude to you. I have my reasons for being the way I am but I should never have taken it out on you. Will you accept my apology?'

He looked desolate, Rowan realised in shock. Like a man who had lost everything with no possibility of ever getting it back. Knowing how that felt, she could more than sympathise.

'Of course.' She replied without hesitation and, as if to underline the words, accompanied them with a smile. A puzzled frown creased Evan's handsome brow.

'Just like that?'

'Why not?'

'You find it so easy to forgive?'

'What's the point in harbouring grudges against people? It only eats you up inside and kills all the joy. Why would I want that for myself?'

'Why indeed?' He found himself smiling back at her, oddly pleased when her shy brown eyes slid away as if she couldn't handle his new-found pleasure in her company. 'I'd better let you get on.'

He went to turn away, planning to lengthen his time spent walking on the beach by an extra twenty minutes. Why not? He was suddenly feeling more optimistic than he had in weeks.

'I was going to offer you a cup of tea,' Rowan

said quickly, 'unless, of course, you think that's taking things a bit too far?'

Noting the suddenly humorous glint in her eyes, Evan found himself warming to the woman more than he believed was sensible. 'A cup of tea would be great—can it wait until I get back from the beach?'

'Sure.' Her heartbeat galloping, Rowan couldn't deny the swift surge of pleasure that invaded her insides at his smiling acceptance. Suddenly, even the prospect of rain that afternoon couldn't dampen her spirits. It's only a cup of tea, she told herself as she watched him stride back down her path onto the road. But it couldn't hurt to offer him a slice of home-made apple pie to go with it, could it?

Negotiating a hallway littered with temporary obstacles of furniture, books and boxes of bric-à-brac, Evan followed an apologetic Rowan into her partly denuded living-room and smiled. 'You look like you mean business,' he commented, glancing around him. All that remained in the room were two small sofas stuffed with a variety of coloured cushions, a sombre Victorian sideboard, an ethnic-looking rug in front of the fireplace and a small portable television set on a stand. The pictures—if she'd had any—had also been removed, because the plain white walls were bare.

'I've never decorated anywhere before, so this is a first for me.' She pushed back her hair and threw him a nervous smile. 'But I'm determined to do it.

The old place needs a bit of tender loving care, wouldn't you say?'

Perching himself on the arm of one of the sofas, Evan rested his hands on his thighs. 'It's been empty for a long time but it looks basically sound to me. Nothing that a few coats of paint and a good spring clean won't solve.'

'Have you owned your cottage long?'

'It was left to me and my sister by our mother ten years ago. She kept it as a holiday home up until she died and we've more or less kept to that tradition. Though it's fair to say that Beth uses it more than I do. She's got two lively boys and they love coming down here for holidays.'

Warmth spread throughout Rowan's insides like butter melting on hot toast. It was the most information the man had voluntarily revealed since she'd met him, and despite his previous animosity she felt strangely privileged. She found herself yearning to know more.

'So you're here on holiday?' she asked, feeling rather disappointed to learn that he wouldn't be her neighbour for long.

The previously thawing expression on Evan's face momentarily froze. 'Something like that.' He shrugged, his lips thinning.

Now Rowan was nonplussed. What exactly did he mean? 'How long are you staying?'

'Three weeks or so...maybe more. I haven't decided.'

'Well, it's certainly a beautiful place to come for a break...however long. Um...would you like tea or coffee? I have both.' Sensing he wasn't exactly conducive to opening up as to why he was staying at the cottage, Rowan decided to steer clear of the subject from now on.

'Tea. Milk, no sugar.' He got up and went to glance out of the window at her bedraggled back garden. 'You've got your work cut out there,' he commented absently.

Hesitating in the kitchen doorway, Rowan released a small sigh. 'I know. Trouble is, what I know about gardening you could write on a postage stamp. I only had a couple of window-boxes in my flat in London and even then I managed to let the poor things that were growing in them die.'

'I'm sure it wasn't intentional.' Leaning back against the window ledge, Evan considered her thoughtfully with those 'you can't hide anything from me' green eyes of his.

A little discomfited by the attention, Rowan hovered in the doorway, wishing she were wearing something a little more feminine than a man's chunky sweater and baggy corduroys that were at least two sizes too big. Even if they were testament to the fact that she had lost quite a bit of weight since Greg had died.

'You're right. It wasn't intentional. Greg and I— that was my husband—were always too busy to do much around the home. Work just demanded too much of our time. Do you know, we were still living out of boxes from our previous flat three years after we moved in because we never found enough time to properly unpack?'

A shadow seemed to pass across Evan's gaze. 'I

can believe it. Work can get you like that sometimes. What did your husband do for a living?'

Rowan automatically smiled. It seemed far easier to talk about Greg than it did about herself to this man, though she couldn't help speculating as to the cause of that deep flash of pain she had just witnessed.

'He was a television cameraman. News mostly. He loved his job—travelled all over the world following stories that were unfolding, in some really inhospitable and dangerous places too. Ironic that he got killed just crossing the road outside our flat.'

Her shoulders drooped a little, it seemed to Evan, and he had a totally uncharacteristic and unexpected desire to run his hand over that silky brown hair of hers and maybe offer comfort in some way. But no sooner had the idea crossed his mind than he scowled inwardly at his own stupidity. How in hell could he comfort anyone? He was a long time bitter, and far too jaded about life to soothe a pretty little widow who had clearly adored her husband and still carried a torch for him.

The timely reminder made him realise he had no business enjoying her company in the first place, and certainly no business sending out wrong signals that he was a much more caring, understanding human being than he really was. If he encouraged their fledgling friendship, sooner or later his bitterness would be bound to taint her in the worst possible way—and Rowan Hawkins did not deserve that after all she'd been through.

'I'm sorry, but I can't stay after all.'

In a flash he'd moved across to the front door before Rowan guessed his intentions.

'Why not?' she demanded without thinking. 'Is it because I told you about Greg? I wasn't looking for your condolences, if that's what you're worried about. I wasn't expecting anything other than a little conversation over a cup of tea.'

Staring into her wide, disingenuous gaze, Evan had the overwhelming sensation that she was pretty much unmarred by the world, despite the awful tragedy that had befallen her. In her soft, liquid brown eyes he saw hope and optimism and, yes, an innocent expectation that life had not yet relinquished its full quota of joy for her. It was almost too much for Evan to bear. All of a sudden he knew an urge to shock, to dispel any hope she might be nurturing about his friendship irrevocably and for good—to make her see that he wasn't fit company for a lovely woman like her.

'And what about my expectations, Rowan?' he fired back at her, mouth twisting.

'What do you mean?' Her soft, pale hand touched her throat.

'What if I find myself wanting more than "a little conversation over a cup of tea"?'

As innocent as she appeared, the gentle flush creeping into her pretty face told Evan that she had undoubtedly understood his meaning in an instant. He wished he could confess to feeling a little shame, but he couldn't because in that instant too he realised that his comment wasn't as far off the mark as he'd believed. He desired her. In fact, right now he'd trade everything he owned to have her in his bed.

CHAPTER FOUR

IT WAS hard to think straight over the sudden roaring in her ears. Something she'd said or done had made him angry, made him want to hit out in some way to hurt her. Rowan recognised pain when she saw it, and self-loathing was startlingly apparent in Evan's raw green gaze as he stood there, clearly wanting to get as far away from her as possible yet at the same time drawn by some underlying instinct that she couldn't fail to register too. Her hand shook a little as she fingered a raised knot of wool on her sweater.

'If you hoped to shock me with your implication then I'm sorry to disappoint you. A cup of tea is all I'm offering, Mr Cameron, and maybe a slice of home-made apple pie. As for anything else...' Her throat threatened to close at this stage, because panic held her prisoner in its grip. When Evan folded his arms across his chest, planting his feet on her mat as if he had no intention of going anywhere in a hurry after all, she almost lost her nerve. 'I'm afraid I'm not in the market for casual liaisons. I was very much in love with my husband, you see, and the fact is, right now, I couldn't contemplate being with another man in that...in that way. I hope we understand each other?'

It was totally incomprehensible to Evan why he should feel such crushing disappointment. He hadn't

51

been remotely attracted to another woman since Rebecca, and after she had done her worst he wasn't in a hurry to get close to another woman again. He'd had flings, yes, here and there. How else was he going to satisfy a healthy libido? But they had all—without exception—only been about sex.

Looking at pretty Rowan Hawkins, with her rosy apple cheeks and her curvy frame hidden beneath her dead husband's baggy sweater and trousers, Evan knew it could never just be about sex with a woman like her. Most men would probably agree she was the kind of woman who had the words 'for ever' imprinted on her soul—the kind of woman you made babies with, then grew old with when the kids had fled the nest. Well, she might not be in the market for 'casual liaisons' but neither was he in the market for 'for ever'. Yet right then he admired the woman more than he could say. She'd handled his outrageous remarks with quiet dignity, and if he owed her an apology before, he surely owed her an even bigger one this time.

'I think we understand each other just fine.' To Rowan's surprise, his lips parted in a self-deprecating little smile. He was outrageously handsome, with a body that wouldn't shame a movie star, and she guessed that not many women would turn down the kind of liaison he'd been hinting at, but then maybe they hadn't loved their partners as much as she'd loved Greg.

'Well, maybe you'd like that cup of tea now?'

'You mentioned apple pie as well?' Evan made an admirable job of disguising his disappointment as his gaze locked and held on to hers. He knew he ought to go, but suddenly he didn't want to return to his empty house, with too many empty hours to fill with unwanted introspection on where his life had gone wrong.

Something in Rowan's heart leapt. She had really thought he would take the escape route he'd deliberately carved for himself and was surprised and more pleased than she had a right to be that he was apparently going to stay. *Shame on you, Rowan Hawkins!*

'Make yourself at home,' she heard herself say. 'I'll make the tea and cut you a slice of pie.'

Somehow an hour had turned into two, and when the sky darkened outside and rain began to splatter against the windows, Rowan ran outside with Evan and brought in her newly drying painted shelves to stand in the hall amongst the other refugees from her living-room.

'Thanks.' Wiping her hand across her damp hair, she wondered whether he'd take the opportunity to bring an end to their cosy little chat. Not that anyone could have called the two hours that had just transpired in any way cosy. There hadn't been much chat either, come to think of it. Evan had wolfed down two slices of pie with gusto, then washed them down with two generous mugs of tea. His appetite taken care of, he'd arranged his fit, hard-muscled frame in one of her dainty little sofas and sat for a long time, not saying anything much at all. Every question Rowan had plucked up the courage to ask him, he'd either answered in as few words as possible or deliberately diverted her with a hard-eyed stare that would have stonewalled any professional interrogator searching for information. The tension in the room had almost become unbearable until the rain had given her a welcome excuse to escape it.

Now she wondered why he was lingering in her hallway, the damp from the rain spreading across his sweatshirt, his expression stark, and strangely she didn't want him to go. Not without learning something about the man that would give her a clue to the conflict going on behind those embittered green eyes of his.

'If you need any help doing anything else round here, let me know.' He pushed his fingers through his curling, damp locks and stared deeply into her upturned face, his suddenly blazing green eyes speaking to her in a language without words. Heat sizzled along Rowan's spine and silently imploded.

'That's nice of you to offer. Thank you.'

'So polite, just like a *good* little girl.'

'It's how my parents brought me up.'

She hated his clearly mocking tone, but heat still engulfed her and made her giddy because she was in such close proximity to him in a confined space that suddenly seemed no bigger than the inside of the blanket box at the end of her bed. There were faint traces of humour in Evan's eyes that told her he probably thought she was kind of quaint—a bit of an oddity, perhaps? Definitely not a woman who understood the kind of sophisticated games that adults could sometimes play.

Good, Rowan thought defiantly, because she

wouldn't want to give the impression she was something she wasn't. If Evan had thought to be nice to her because it had suddenly occurred to him that she might prove a handy diversion whilst he stayed at the cottage, then he had another think coming. She was going to be nobody's port in a storm—least of all for an angry, embittered man who couldn't even trouble himself to make half-decent conversation with another human being.

But something was happening between them. Something that, once realised, couldn't be denied. This something seemed to fill up the space between them and made it hard to breathe. Now Rowan's gaze was fixed on the impossibly sexy cleft in the centre of Evan's chin and the two little shaving nicks he'd made beside it, and the words she tried to form in her brain wouldn't seem to make the necessary journey to her lips.

'You'd better go.'

'I think perhaps I'd better.' Reaching out, he tugged a sleek, curling tendril beside her cheek and for a moment his knuckle grazed her skin, stirring the air into living electricity around them. 'Thanks for the tea. The apple pie was great too.'

When the front door closed behind him, Rowan put her hands up to her burning face and breathed deeply into them. 'Oh, God...'

For a whole week Evan managed to avoid his distracting neighbour. When he saw her digging in the garden or setting out for a walk or returning in her car from a shopping trip, he told himself it was none of his business what she got up to, that he should just concentrate his energies on getting back to full fitness. At least his appetite had returned. But thinking of food automatically made him think about Rowan's heavenly apple pie, and then naturally that led to him thinking about the woman herself.

It was too cruel what had happened to her husband. It didn't seem right that a woman like her should be on her own. If Evan's intuition was right, she had a nurturing instinct a mile wide and by rights should have a brood of happy, noisy kids to take care of by now. How old must she be? Twenty-nine? Thirty?

He was too restless to sit, so Evan's long legs carried him to the window overlooking Rowan's garden. The lady had been busy, he saw. She'd mown the wild grass and dug over the borders and an old green wheelbarrow stood to the side with two sacks of compost in it. The weather had turned appreciably warmer today and he speculated whether she'd be tempted to don that white dress of hers, along with that ridiculous straw hat. His lips twisted in derision. Why on earth should she, when he'd been so disparaging about her wearing them the first time they had met?

About to turn away, Evan stood perfectly still as Rowan suddenly came into view. She carried a big aluminum watering-can that water sploshed out of as she walked, and she was wearing old jeans, a white T-shirt and green Wellington boots that looked at least two sizes too big. If it weren't for those distinctly feminine curves, she'd have reminded him of a little girl lost in a world of her own, oblivious to anything else going on around her but the task she'd set herself.

Before he even had time to question the wisdom of what he was about to do, Evan strode back across his living-room, then out into the hallway to his front door.

Enjoying the feel of the sun on her back as she liberally watered her newly sown plants, Rowan barely glanced up as she heard the front gate squeak open. Lost in thought, she couldn't quell the growing sense of satisfaction that was taking root inside her at just how much she'd managed to accomplish both in the house and the garden this week. She'd been sleeping better too, because her body had been so physically tired by the time she crawled into bed each night that she'd fallen asleep almost as soon as her head touched the pillow.

When the sound of the doorbell permeated her musing, Rowan glanced round in shock, her heart-beat skidding like a roller skater heading for a fall. It couldn't be who she thought it was, could it? It was obvious that Evan had deliberately kept out of her way since that provoking little encounter in her hallway a week ago, and she told herself she was glad. What business did she want with a man who was clearly exorcising demons of his own, who seemed to find it hard to tolerate the company of another human being, let alone ordinary conversation?

She took a deep breath, then silently counted to ten before unlocking the front door.

'I thought you might need some help.'

It seemed typical of the man that he casually waded right in, as though a whole week hadn't just gone by without them so much as wishing each other good morning. Clamping down her surge of irritation, Rowan wiped her hands down the thighs of her jeans then tucked her hair behind her ears. Despite his apparent disregard for the usual conventions, she couldn't help being overwhelmed by the mere sight of him. Even dressed casually as he was, in a dark blue sweatshirt and black jeans, Evan Cameron was a disconcerting force of nature that knocked her sideways. All that powerful masculinity contained in a hard, lean body honed to awesome perfection was enough to make a grown woman weep. Now where had that thought come from? Guiltily, her brown eyes shied away from direct confrontation with his.

'I'm—I'm fine, thanks.'

'Could you use some help or couldn't you?' Leaning against the door jamb, Evan didn't look as if he intended to let her brush him off so easily.

'What sort of help are you offering, Mr Cameron?' Thinking about all the work that needed doing in her presently emptied front room, Rowan was having second thoughts about refusing his assistance so abruptly. Just yesterday the industrial sander she'd hired to do the downstairs floors had arrived, but as she was in the middle of working on the garden she'd decided that the floors would have to wait until she was ready.

'I can turn my hand to most things. Whatever a lady needs a man around the house for, I can do.'

He shrugged, then grinned unrepentantly, his green eyes suddenly acquiring a devilish gleam at Rowan's helpless blush. Clearing her throat, she stepped back into the hallway to indicate he should come in. 'Actually, you might have called at a most opportune moment. How are you at sanding floors?'

It was worth clogging up his lungs with dust for the day to be rewarded with a mug of tea and a generous, mouthwatering slice of Rowan's home-made cherry pie, Evan concluded as he took a break with her in the small galley kitchen. They'd closed the door to prevent wood-dust coating everything else, and Evan sat at the pine table in the alcove watching Rowan as she busily wiped down surfaces then straightened the cookery books on the small wooden shelf on the window-ledge as though her hands couldn't keep still.

'I think I've become addicted to your baking,' he commented, licking a small splurge of cherry juice off his thumb. Transfixed by the sight, Rowan slowly let out her breath and stopped what she was doing.

'Home cooking is always nicer—whether it's cordon bleu or just plain old bangers and mash. Did your wife—?' Stricken by her bad *faux pas*, Rowan covered her mouth with her hand. At the table, Evan took an outwardly calm sip of tea before replying.

'Rebecca didn't cook much. She was far too busy employing her dubious talents elsewhere.' Like his best friend's bed, Evan grimly recalled. His gaze settled thoughtfully on Rowan. The poor woman looked as if she wanted the ground to open up and swallow her. He knew he had to put her out of her misery. It wasn't her fault that his wife had had the morals of an alley cat—not to mention the claws too, sharp enough to put him off marriage for life, in fact. 'Don't give her another thought. Believe me, she isn't worth it.' Getting to his feet, he reached for the door-handle, but Rowan stopped him in his tracks.

'She—she must have hurt you badly. You seem so…bitter.' Her softly shaped brows drew together as if she couldn't bear to contemplate a husband or wife being cruel to their spouse. It almost made Evan want to shield her from the harsher realities of life…almost, but not quite.

'Rebecca was a clever, manipulative woman who used men to get what she wanted in life. When I cottoned on to her…not so admirable qualities, shall we say?—she moved on to my best friend. I only found out later, after she'd got the courts to award her most of my assets, that she'd done the same thing to another poor jerk before me.' Briefly dipping his head, Evan let go of the door-handle. Rowan could almost see the tension that locked his back and shoulders. It took a supreme effort on her part not to reach out and massage that tension away. She came to her senses with a shock at what she'd actually contemplated doing.

'But how did she get the court to award her most of your assets?' she heard herself ask instead.

'She was pregnant at the time our divorce was petitioned. She swore the baby was mine.'

'And it—it wasn't?'

'No, it wasn't. And her lawyer argued a convincing case so that she didn't have to submit to tests to prove it.' With a dark glower Evan grimly moved his head from side to side, then wrenched open the door. 'I'd better get back to sanding the rest of that floor. Another hour, I'd say, and the job will be done.'

She knew she ought to know better, but Rowan followed him out into the living-room just the same. The windows were thrown wide open to help disperse the dust and the sun poured in to illuminate every beautiful sanded floorboard. Evan had worked hard and she was immensely grateful. Up until a few moments ago in the kitchen he'd seemed to relax into an almost companionable silence with her, but now he was angry and tense and Rowan wished she knew a way to restore some harmony between them. How could his wife have cheated on him? she wondered. Evan Cameron was surely more than enough man for most women?

'Did you want children?'

'What?' His green eyes flashed a warning, as if she had already gone too far, but Rowan determinedly stood her ground. No wound left to fester ever healed, and it didn't take a psychotherapist to deduce that that was exactly what Evan had been allowing his emotional wounds to do.

'I asked if you wanted children.'

The question cut him to the quick. He remembered the joy he'd experienced when Rebecca had come back that afternoon from the doctor's...the plans he'd made about buying them a bigger house, upgrading her car to the latest model with all those brand-new hi-tech safety features... His gut clenched as though deflecting a blow.

'The subject isn't up for discussion.' Grimly he strode towards the sander, where he had left it, then reached across to the mantelpiece to retrieve his protective mask.

Rowan steeled herself. 'I'm sorry that your wife hurt you so badly and that—and that the baby wasn't yours. But you're a young, attractive man and there'll be other relationships. Hopefully one day you'll find someone who truly loves you for yourself and you can have all the children you want. One thing I've learned is that we must never let the pain of the past blind us to the possibilities of the future.'

'Quite the little philosopher, aren't you?' Turning on her, Evan drew the paper mask in his fist into a tight ball. 'What would you know of betrayal, hmm? You, with your no doubt perfect marriage to Mr Wonderful? Just keep your misguided sympathies out of my business, Rowan, and let me deal with my life in my own way.'

Switching on the sander, he drowned out further discussion with the noise, leaving Rowan with no option other than to make her way back out into the garden to tend to her plants.

Had she had a perfect marriage? Crouching low over some bulbs she was planting, Rowan scratched her head and sighed. Greg had been a wonderful partner, a warm, funny, insightful and caring man who'd never given her one moment's cause to regret marrying him. But their marriage hadn't been perfect. How could it have been? How could anyone's? They'd had their ups and downs like everyone else; regrets too. For instance, how often had they put off having a child of their own in deference to furthering their careers? Well...*his* career in particular. Rowan absorbed the little niggle of resentment in her chest and shook her head.

Her thoughts ran on. How many nights had she spent alone when Greg had been abroad, filming some insurgent uprising or war? How many times had she feared for his life in those anxious situations? And yet he'd come home after every one, thrilled to see her but just as eager to be off again to some other potentially explosive situation in some remote part of the world—thousands of miles away from his lonely wife. Had she been lonely? God, yes. No matter how many times Greg had gone away, she'd never quite got used to it. Many were the nights Rowan had cried herself to sleep because she'd missed her husband, yearned for him to be there with her in their cosy little flat, longed for him in their bed...

Heat seeped up her neck and into her cheeks. Why did men think they were the only ones who had needs? Just because she was a widow now, it didn't mean she was suddenly dead from the waist down, did it? Her throat tightened and she impatiently started to dig again with the little green trowel. Damn Evan Cameron and his surly ways. No wonder his wife had left him for someone else if that was how he'd carried on! Swallowing down her hurt, she let go of the trowel and eased up onto her feet. A wave of remorse washed over her. She shouldn't say that. It was plain that he was a man in an immense amount of pain. Only hurt people were angry. It made Rowan wonder what he had been like before the betrayal.

She sighed. If only he could learn to smile a bit more, to laugh, if only—

'Rowan.'

He appeared at the back door, hands on hips, handsome face unsmiling and pensive. Rowan's heart sank to her boots.

'What is it?'

'Want to come round to my place for a bite to eat tonight?'

His question floored her. She stared. 'I—I...'

'Don't get too excited...it's only stir-fry.'

'Well, I—what time do you want me round?' she heard herself ask, and couldn't suppress the leap of inexplicable hope in her chest.

'Eight o'clock is fine.'

'Want me to bring dessert?'

'Any cherry pie left?' Evan grinned back.

Rowan nodded, an answering smile tugging at her mouth that just wouldn't be tamped. 'Plenty. I'll bring some home-made custard as well.'

'You're a dangerous woman, Rowan Hawkins... anyone ever tell you that?'

Her toes were still curling as he turned and went inside.

CHAPTER FIVE

IN DEFERENCE to Rowan's visit, Evan put a cloth on the table and lit a candle. Then, thinking better of such an uncharacteristic impulse, he blew out the candle and shoved the little brass holder back into a cupboard. What was he thinking of? And what on earth had possessed him to invite the woman to dinner? As soon as the invitation was out of his mouth he'd regretted it. Her sherry-brown eyes had gone from sad to hopeful in an instant, and that wasn't what Evan had planned at all. What he'd planned on doing was keeping Rowan Hawkins at a distance until he went back to London. But now—unless he took another deliberate U-turn and alienated the woman even more—he'd have to extend the hand of friendship indefinitely, at least while he was staying at the cottage.

Briefly leaning his head against the wall, he tried desperately to gain some sense of control over what was happening. All along he'd told himself he didn't need company. Nor did he need comfort, come to that, and certainly not from a woman who could surely use a little of that commodity herself.

He straightened, staring at the sizeable wok he'd placed on the unlit stove and the assorted dishes of vegetables and herbs he'd chopped up and placed in readiness on the counter beside it. He glanced at the clock on the kitchen wall, registering that it was just after eight, then lifted his hands to examine them. No shakes… That was good. Thank God for small mercies. So he'd cook the meal he'd planned, offer her a glass of wine, make a little light conversation as best he could, then hopefully once they'd eaten she'd take the hint and not outstay her welcome. Perhaps he wouldn't have to encourage her friendship after all in that case. Why not just let her think he was moody and unpredictable? Heaven knew it wasn't far from the truth. Then from tomorrow onwards Evan could affect a little more distance again. Maybe tell her he was going to be busy for the next couple of weeks and do his best to keep a low profile. Confident he had things under control again, he switched on the radio and turned to the cooker.

She came into his house like a princess bearing gifts, a creamy pashmina shawl draped around her shoulders over a long white calico dress, her arms full of plastic storage boxes and a bottle of wine. After instructing him on the heating procedure for the pie and the custard, she turned a becoming shade of pink when he merely grinned and relieved her of her booty, then became suddenly silent as Evan placed everything on the counter and turned back to study her. Her delicate fragrance wafted round her, filling his nostrils and invading his senses with pleasure as though he stood in an orchard somewhere with the scent of new-mown grass and sunlight warming his back. Relaxing his gaze and folding his arms across his chest, he was in no hurry to sully the magical moment with needless conversation.

Heat prickled all the way down Rowan's spine as Evan studied her, and it felt as though every part of her body suddenly became much too sensitive. She pulled her shawl more securely around her shoulders and attempted a smile. She'd had her doubts about coming to his house and now his unsettling behaviour merely confirmed them. Why was he looking at her like that? Didn't he like what she was wearing? If only he'd known how she'd anguished as to what to put on, anxious not to make it look as if she wanted to please him in some way with her appearance—to somehow set the tone just right. Now she knew she must have got it wrong. Back in London she frequented antique shops and the stalls in Camden Market for her clothing, and her style, if she had one, was probably what might be termed a little old-fashioned—Laura Ashley meets hippy chick. Greg had claimed to love it, but Evan Cameron, with his steely, toned biceps and fierce green eyes, clearly didn't.

'I'm sorry I'm a little late,' She made a show of glancing at her watch, feeling herself redden like a schoolgirl. 'I was trying to find something to wear that wasn't covered in wood dust!'

'You look just fine to me,' Evan drawled. Still he didn't move.

Rowan fanned herself. 'It's very warm in here, isn't it? Can I do anything? Something smells nice.'

Too late, she took a step towards the cooker, then found herself trapped by the unwavering directness of his stare.

'I've got it all under control,' he said quietly, voice low.

'You have?' Rowan stared, then reluctantly dragged her gaze away to look anywhere but straight at him. The man was tying her up in knots with his examination. What was he trying to do to her?

'How about a glass of wine?'

'Thanks. Yes.'

Relieved, she gulped down a deep breath, letting it out slowly as Evan turned back to the counter. Free at last from his disturbing gaze, she allowed herself a quick study of the warm, homely kitchen, with its neat pine units and framed watercolours of children playing on a beach all round the walls. The large refrigerator was covered in childish fridge magnets—Tom and Jerry, and characters from the *The Simpsons*. There were a couple of drawings—a robot and a spaceship—lovingly signed for 'Uncle Evan'. Rowan deduced they must be the output of the two nephews he'd mentioned. Were they close to their brooding, taciturn uncle? The thought intrigued her. Was it possible for anyone to get close to this man?

'What are you thinking?' he asked as he turned round and placed a glass of chilled white wine into her hands.

'I was just admiring your nephews' drawings. Do you get to see much of them?'

'Not really.' Evan admitted it with a pang. He'd always been too busy working. Now and then he'd show up at birthdays or Christmas with a couple of expensive gifts that his secretary had purchased on his behalf, but other than that he was conspicuous in their lives by his absence. He took a sip of wine and shrugged. It was just as well that Beth didn't hold it against him, but it pained him to realise he probably didn't deserve her to be so magnanimous.

'They're great kids but I don't get to see them as much as I'd like.'

'It's never too late,' Rowan commented, her smile sunny.

Heat attacked Evan from all sides. That damn smile of hers was dangerous…didn't she have the sense to bestow it more wisely? 'Yeah, you're probably right. Want to sit down and eat?'

Savouring her wine, feeling its initial chill turn to warmth in her belly, Rowan picked up her cutlery and twirled some noodles around her fork. 'This smells good. You obviously enjoy cooking.'

'Good food is important. It gives you vitality and energy.' Two things he'd had in short supply lately, Evan reflected as he considered his plate. It wasn't the answer Rowan had somehow expected. Clearly good nutrition meant a lot to him. No wonder he looked in such good shape: he obviously took great care of himself.

'That's true, but when you're too busy working it's not always easy to organise the best food. It becomes all too easy to pop something instant into the microwave…though I never did that too often myself. I mainly had to do it for Greg when he came home unexpectedly—sometimes in the middle of the small hours.'

'So…what did you do when your husband was away?'

'I was working a lot myself.' She tasted some food, chewed it, then swallowed before glancing directly up at Evan. He was watching her with that slow, probing gaze of his that made her skin far too sensitive, and suddenly the room seemed terrifyingly smaller. 'By the time I'd got home in the evening, got myself something to eat then sorted out my clothes for the morning, I was too tired to contemplate doing much else...though I did do an aerobics class once a week. Nearly killed me too.' She grinned and her brown eyes went soft with merriment.

Once again, heat stirred low in Evan's stomach, making him ache for her in a way that would surely make her pretty cheeks pinker than they were already if she even had a hint of how he was feeling.

Irritated that he wasn't as in control of his emotions as he'd like, he pushed away from the table abruptly and moved across to the counter to make coffee. 'I suppose once a week is better than nothing, but it's not a good idea to throw yourself into doing something as energetic as aerobics if you're not taking any other form of exercise. You can easily injure yourself if your muscles aren't properly warmed up. What do you do for a living?'

Staring at his back, helplessly contemplating his arresting physique in blue denims and a black shirt, Rowan patted her lips with her paper napkin and strove to get her galloping pulse under control. 'I was a production assistant in an independent television company.'

'Was?'

He paused from spooning coffee grounds into the cafetière and turned round to look at her. Her slender shoulders rose and fell with a little shrug of what appeared to be dejection. 'I gave it up to come and live here.'

'So how are you going to support yourself?'

Rowan flinched at his bluntness. No skirting round the issue for politeness' sake, obviously. 'I'll be fine for a year or so. I want to—I need to take some time to think about what I want to do next.'

Evan said nothing, then turned back to make the coffee. Did he think she was wrong to take time out? Perhaps he thought she was running away. Worse still, lazy.

'So, if aerobics isn't a good idea, any suggestions what I can do to get fit?'

Her comment provoked a surprising grin. 'Stick to your gardening and DIY, is my suggestion. A few regular walks on the beach wouldn't go amiss either. What do you want to get fit for, Rowan?'

Putting down her fork, she folded her napkin carefully beside it. 'Sometimes I feel like I've been hit by a ten-ton truck, you know? I wake up in the morning and feel like I just want to stay in bed. That scares me. If I were fitter I'd have more energy and could apply myself better...that's all.'

Her first couple of comments could easily have applied to him, Evan thought grimly. But he knew, with Rowan, her fatigue was due to grief. A stab of remorse tightened his chest.

'If you want me to help you get fitter, I will.' Bringing the coffee-pot to the table, along with two dark blue ceramic mugs, Evan sat down opposite her. He saw the surprise in her face. Then her delectable mouth curved into a sweet smile that made him want her again in the most inappropriate way.

'You will?'

'It's what I do for a living,' he explained. 'Helping people to get fit is my business.'

'It is?'

Irritation flashed in his suddenly cool green eyes. 'Don't you believe me?' Could she tell? he wondered. Did she know he was all washed up? A fitness instructor who could no longer take a simple walk on the beach without breaking into a sweat, let alone attempt anything more strenuous. His hand curved around the handle of his fork and squeezed tight.

Rowan saw his knuckles turn briefly white and couldn't fathom what she'd said to offend him. 'Of course I believe you; why wouldn't I? I only need to look at your body and I—and I…' She went the colour of a ripe tomato.

Evan relaxed his death grip on the fork and let it go. Amusement replacing irritation, he leant back in his chair to study her. 'You look at my body and…tell me, Rowan.'

'Well.' She picked up her napkin and refolded it. 'What I meant to say was, you look as though you take care of yourself.'

'And what about you?' he coaxed softly.

'What about me?'

'Do you take care of your body too?'

'I know I'm a little out of shape right now.' Embarrassed, she glanced away from him, her soft brown hair falling across her cheek as she bent her head.

She was so wrong. He remembered the red sweater and jeans she'd had on that day. It had revealed a shape more than a little pleasing to the eye. Evan had taken one look at her and felt as horny as hell.

'How can I tell when you insist on hiding yourself beneath those long, baggy dresses of yours?'

'They're not baggy!' Stung, she faced him with a furious glare. 'They're…tasteful. I don't think a woman should reveal everything about herself, do you? I think she should retain a little—a little mystery.'

Personally, Evan agreed. It made the conquest all the sweeter. Only he'd never met a woman yet who had felt the same. Rebecca had had an amazing body and her tight, figure-hugging clothes had made no pretence at concealing it. He couldn't deny that he hadn't minded being the envy of every other man in the room when he walked in with her. But now the very thought of her left him cold. The pretty young woman sitting opposite him, with her shy smile and her demure dress, was a million miles away from someone like his ex-wife, and Evan found he was intensely comforted by the thought. Comforted, yet still turned on by the idea of peeling away the protective layers of clothing to reveal the lovely woman underneath, because he knew instinctively that was just what she would be…

'You were never tempted to stray when your husband was away?' he found himself asking her.

'Of course not!'

Allowing her gaze to linger on that hard, slightly arrogant mouth of his, Rowan felt heat throb through her body. Where was he heading with such a question? Was he suggesting that she was a woman who missed the intimacy of a man sharing her bed so much that she would do anything to satisfy needs that weren't being met? Did he think that she expected him to—wanted him to...? Impatient with herself, she glanced hopefully towards the coffee-pot. *No more wine, Rowan. A couple of sips and you're getting the kind of ideas that won't do you a bit of good in the long run.* Clearly Evan Cameron was just playing with her. Stringing her along for his own perverse amusement. He wasn't a bit attracted to her, she decided. A man who had the kind of outstanding good looks that he possessed, and was a fitness instructor to boot, wouldn't waste his time on someone as plain and ordinary as her. Someone who hid their body rather than revealed it, who talked about retaining mystery in the twenty-first century when revealing less was definitely not more.

'I didn't mean to offend you.'

'You haven't. Do you mind if I have some coffee now?'

'You're not going to finish your meal?'

'I'm suddenly...not very hungry. Do you mind?' Her brown eyes round with apology, she flushed. Shaking his head, Evan gave a rueful grin. 'I guess I'll have to live with the fact you don't like my cooking.'

When she bit her lip and flushed again, he chuckled. Clearly even the thought of offending anyone was pure torture to her. 'Only kidding. Let's take the coffee through to the living-room, shall we?'

Settled in a big leather armchair, her cup of coffee cradled in her hands, Rowan glanced towards the crackling fire in the old-fashioned hearth and willed herself to relax. Resigned to the fact that she obviously wasn't Evan's type, she told herself they might still be friends. If only the man would open up to her a little more. If only he could learn to trust her. She would never betray a friend's confidence—if she could just convince him of that, they might get somewhere.

'So when can you start helping me to get fit?' she asked as he strode past her with his coffee. Settling himself on an ottoman by the hearth, his green eyes reflecting little sparks of flame from the fire, Evan took a few moments to answer her. Was he regretting offering his services? Rowan worried. He was probably thinking now he'd never get rid of her! The last thing in the world she wanted to be was a nuisance.

'Tomorrow morning. Be ready by six and we'll go for a power walk on the beach—maybe do a little gentle stretching first to get warmed up.'

'At six o'clock in the morning? Are you serious?'

'Perhaps I ought to be asking you that question?'

'All right.' Feeling as if she'd definitely bitten off more than she could chew, Rowan flashed him a weak smile. 'But don't expect miracles. I told you I'm actually not in very good shape.'

'We'll see.' His expression implacable, Evan shrugged as he raised his cup of coffee thoughtfully to his lips.

*   *   *

His knock on her door the following morning found Rowan still struggling to undo a knot in the lace of one of her little-used trainers. Standing back to allow him entry, she glimpsed the dawn breaking behind him and helplessly shivered. What was she doing, for goodness' sake? She'd come to the cottage to retreat from the rat race, not to rise at some ungodly hour to 'power walk' on the beach with a man who looked as if he could give an Olympic sprinter a run for his money!

'Ready?'

By the determined set of that hard jaw of his, Evan meant business. Attired in black sweats and a navy-blue fleece, the man emanated energy and electricity in equally potent doses. A small surge of trepidation shot through her. She really did believe that getting a little fitter would help her, not just physically but mentally too—but, glancing at Evan, she was definitely having second thoughts. The man looked simply awesome.

'As ready as I'll ever be.'

'Good. Then we'll get started.'

Instead of heading out through the door, he led the way back into Rowan's still emptied living-room. Standing on the newly sanded floorboards, he proceeded to take her through a series of warm-up exercises to 'get her blood pumping'. Feeling perspiration start to gather on her brow, Rowan tried to coax tired, stiff muscles into submission, all the while keeping one eye on Evan as he stretched effortlessly and smoothly, her heart tripping at the sight of that heavenly body on display purely for her benefit. *If my friends could see me now,* she mused in a fit of amusement, *they really would think I'd flipped.*

'Come on, Rowan, you're not concentrating.'

You try concentrating in my position, she mentally retaliated, wondering if the man had the faintest inkling of how arresting he was. With his black hair, smouldering green eyes and a body to kill for, was there a woman alive who couldn't help but be distracted by him?

'I'm doing my best here.' Reaching down to touch her toes, she almost passed out when Evan came up behind her and put his hands on her back.

'Tuck your tailbone in. You'll hurt yourself doing it like that.'

Feeling all the blood in her body rush to her head, Rowan quickly straightened, spinning round to face him with her hair escaping from her pony-tail in all directions, telling herself she was mad to have even imagined she could do this. Be here, with *him* like this.

'Isn't that enough stretching for now?' Shoving her hair out of her eyes, she yanked down the pink stretch top that had ridden up to her waist.

Depends on how you look at it, Evan thought wryly, catching a glimpse of her cute belly button. In all his years as an instructor at gyms round the country, he'd never been so aroused by seeing a woman work out as he was now with Rowan. That curvy little body of hers was even more of a turn-on than he'd first suspected. She was probably right. It was time to go outside. Another moment alone with her in that empty room and he'd be suggesting they work out in a different way entirely.

'Yeah, that's probably enough. Let's go down to the beach.'

'Good idea.'

She was out of the door in a flash of pink and grey before Evan had even blinked. Grinning, because he knew she'd been as affected by the electricity generated between them as he had, he quickly followed her, intrigued to find out just how she proposed to deal with it.

CHAPTER SIX

AFTER walking on the beach for nearly half an hour, Evan realised with no small sense of shock that he wasn't feeling the slightest bit winded or in difficulty. As he strode alongside Rowan, encouraging her to concentrate on her rhythm and breathing as they upped the pace, he cautiously admitted to himself that he was actually enjoying the experience. How long had it been since he had been able to say that in all honesty? Glancing at the woman beside him, her soft brown hair blowing in the breeze, her brow furrowed in deep concentration, doing her level best to keep step with his naturally longer stride, he experienced a spurt of pleasure that almost made his lips quirk into a grin. He thought he'd made a mistake in offering to help her get fit, but now he wasn't so sure.

'It's certainly bracing, isn't it?' Turning to him, she let loose a smile, her cheeks pink and glowing, her face naturally beautiful without a scrap of make-up, and Evan wondered how he had ever found that high-maintenance look, which most of his previous girl-friends and Rebecca had favoured, remotely attractive.

'Next you'll be telling me you're enjoying it.'

'But I am!' She laughed uninhibitedly—a happy almost childlike sound that blew away on the wind. 'Isn't this amazing? It feels like we're the only two people on earth!'

As she gazed ahead at the infinite stretch of sand turning to gold beneath the early-morning sun, the tide rushing in beside them as they walked, the heart-ache that was never normally far away seemed to recede and Rowan realised she was feeling happier than she had in ages.

'So, you want to do this again tomorrow?' Raising his voice above the crash of the surf, Evan grinned.

Be still, my poor, beating heart… Rowan thought silently beside him.

'Bring it on!' Laughing out loud, she deliberately broke into a run, letting loose a wild whoop as she pounded across the sand. Behind her, Evan stopped smiling. He suddenly knew he was in deep trouble…*emotional* trouble. The kind he'd sworn to avoid like the plague.

'So you'll come?'

'But, Jane, a party?'

'Yeah. Dreadful, isn't it?'

In spite of her deep reservations about going to London for the weekend and attending a party where she would inevitably bump into one or two friends of both hers and Greg's, Rowan had to smile. Since her power walk on the beach this morning with Evan her spirits had remained optimistically high. It had given her a sense of wonder and strength, a belief that maybe she could achieve things she usually avoided out of fear. Greg was gone. Nothing on this earth was ever going to bring him back. She had to get on with her life. Not be afraid. Have fun. He surely wouldn't have begrudged her that?

'All right. I'll chuck a few clothes into a bag and be at your place about six this evening. Party or not, it'll be good to catch up. You can tell me all about this new man of yours. Will he be there tomorrow night?'

'Of course.'

Hearing the smile in her friend's voice, Rowan couldn't help but be delighted for Jane. Having just turned thirty, convinced she was destined to remain single for the rest of her natural life, she had recently met Andrew, the man of her dreams—in a doctor's waiting room, if you please. Rowan couldn't wait to hear the full story.

'I know it hasn't been easy for you, Rowan—God, that must be the understatement of the year! But I really think it would do you good to come up to London for a while. I've missed you. One thing's for sure—work is a duller place for your absence.'

'I miss it sometimes too,' Rowan conceded, raking her fingers through her hair, 'but I'm loving it where I am. One weekend soon you and Andrew must come down for a visit. Trust me, you won't want to leave.'

'I'll take your word for it. Personally I wouldn't want to be stuck out in the middle of nowhere with just myself for company. Don't you get even the slightest bit lonely?'

Her mind gravitating helplessly to her handsome next-door neighbour, Rowan chewed down guiltily on her lip. 'No,' she said firmly, even knowing he wouldn't be there forever. 'I don't get lonely at all.'

*   *   *

'We'll have to postpone our beach walk till Monday,' she told him, dark eyes sliding guiltily away. 'I'm going up to London to stay with a friend for a couple of days.'

Disappointment was fierce. Evan felt it deep in his gut, like a piece of bad news he didn't want to hear. Distracted for a moment by the loud squawking of a passing gull, he shielded his gaze with his hand from the sharp glare of the sun before levelling it back down to Rowan. 'Spontaneous decision, was it?' he asked casually.

Meeting the impenetrable barrier of his glance and feeling a sharp tug of something that resembled regret, Rowan heaved a sigh. 'You could say that, yes.'

'Country life must be beginning to pall, then.'

'Not at all. I've got friends in London I haven't seen for a while and I've been invited to a party, that's all.'

There was no earthly reason why Evan should feel apprehensive about that, but he did. Along with a strange feeling of foreboding that he shrugged off as just his imagination, in the deep silence of his mind he had to admit he didn't want her to go. Now that he'd got used to seeing her around, the weekend would be interminable—knowing she wasn't pottering about next door, valiantly experimenting with her DIY or tending her rambling back garden.

'A party, hmm?' His singularly unimpressed tone told her that it was the last thing in the world he would want to contemplate. Still, something perverse made her ask the question.

'You could come too if you wanted. My friend has a large flat. I'm sure she wouldn't mind if you stayed. I've got a spare sleeping bag somewhere, if you don't mind sleeping on the floor. I mean, I—that is if you…'

Her heart thumped as he slowly folded his arms across that impressive chest of his and fixed her with the most lustful stare she'd ever experienced in her life.

'You inviting me to come and share a sleeping bag with you, Rowan?'

Heat stung her cheeks. 'I didn't say that. You know very well I wasn't inviting you to do any such thing!'

'I don't go to parties,' he said clearly, then started to turn away. 'Not any more.'

All of a sudden Rowan wished she hadn't told Jane she would go. The idea that Evan would spend the weekend on his own, with no one to talk to or even pass the time of day with, filled her with deep regret. She knew him well enough now to know that he would immediately insist that he preferred his own company anyway if she so much as hinted he would be lonely on his own, but still the feeling that she was somehow abandoning him lingered. Pushing her hair out of her eyes, Rowan searched frantically for a way to make him stay on his doorstep a little longer.

'I really enjoyed our exercise session this morning. I'm probably going to ache like God knows what tomorrow, but for the first time in ages I really felt alive, you know?'

Evan did know. He had felt it too, but unlike Rowan he didn't put it down to the exercise alone.

'Exercise can do that for you. As long as you don't take it to extremes.' Shame he didn't know how to take his own advice…

'I doubt if I'd do that. I'm not an extreme kind of person. Slow and plodding, that's me.'

Suddenly Evan experienced a raw stab of anger at himself, at his sorry inability to take heed of his own cautionary warnings not to get involved with a woman ever again except in the most basic way. Because when he gazed at beguiling Rowan Hawkins, with her glossy brown hair and shining dark eyes full of hope and optimism, he wanted something that he knew would only bring him more heartache and pain. Best he sever any hope of that right now before things went any further. He'd keep his promise to help her get fit, but other than that he would keep contact strictly to an impersonal minimum.

'Well.' Rubbing his hand round the back of his neck, he gave her a brief, cursory nod. 'You'd best get going. It's a long drive to London. Drive safely.' And with that, he turned around and went inside, shutting the door firmly behind him.

She'd forgotten how noisy people could be. Jane's production manager's house, where the party was being held, was large and rambling, with lofty ceilings and revitalised Victorian grandeur. But even so, with humanity spilling out of practically every room, Rowan was beginning to feel a bit like a cornered rabbit, hemmed in as she was by a couple of girl-friends and Jane's affable new boyfriend, Andrew. She strained to keep the drift of the conversation as music boomed out from strategically placed speakers, unable to suppress a sudden, almost desperate longing for the peace and quiet of her little cottage near the sea.

'You're a brave woman, hiding yourself away down there in the wilds of Pembrokeshire,' Andrew was saying, his friendly blue eyes smiling down into hers. 'Don't you miss the buzz of living in the city?'

Rowan had no hesitation in her reply. 'No, I honestly don't. You can't imagine how wonderful it is to just wake up to the sound of birdsong and seagulls crying, and the wind rattling the windows. And the smell in the air is something else! So clean and fresh and unpolluted. As far as I'm concerned there's just no contest.'

'So you've no plans to come back to London anytime soon?'

Her brown eyes were emphatic as she cradled her wine glass. 'Definitely not. I'm quite happy where I am, thank you. And you and Jane must come for a visit soon.' *But not too soon…*

Her smile was particularly bright because the stray thought coming out of nowhere made her feel foolishly guilty. But Rowan told herself she was thinking of Evan as well. The last thing the man wanted was strangers tramping all over the place when he had gone down there in search of peace and quiet. She wondered vaguely what he was doing right now. Perhaps reading one of those thrillers she'd seen piled up on his coffee-table, or taking a walk on the beach on his own? She experienced an inordinate pang of longing to be there with him. Oh, why had she let Jane persuade her to come to this noisy, smoky party when she'd much rather be at home?

After establishing that Rowan wasn't hungry, the girls departed in search of nibbles from the generously supplied dining area. Andrew lingered for a few minutes longer until he spied Jane entering the room, then excused himself to go and talk to her. Taking an absent-minded sip of her wine, Rowan backed up against the window and perched herself on its glossed white ledge with a relieved sigh. Glancing at her watch, she saw the time was a little after eleven. If she were at home now she'd be snuggled up in bed with a good book or listening to late-night radio.

'Well, well...what a surprise! If it isn't my old friend Greg's pretty little wife, Rowan. How are you? You remember me, don't you?'

Matthew Napier. The one colleague of Greg's that she had never really got along with. Opinionated and arrogant, he had a knack of rubbing people up the wrong way. As Rowan tried to summon up a smile, she looked into his leering pale grey eyes and prayed for someone to take pity and come and rescue her soon. But Jane was preoccupied with Andrew and her other friends had disappeared off somewhere else in the rambling house, so it would be down to Rowan herself to come up with a quick getaway plan.

'Matthew...of course I remember you.' Self-consciously she moved her hands to the modestly low neckline of her silk floral dress and tried to raise it a little, so as not to expose too much creamy, smooth flesh to this man's lascivious gaze.

'Dreadful about what happened to poor old Greg, wasn't it?'

Obviously when God had been handing out tact and discretion, Matthew Napier must have been at the back of the queue.

'I'd rather not talk about that, if you don't mind.'

'So what are you doing with yourself these days? I haven't seen you around for quite some time.'

Deliberately moving in closer, Matthew took a generous slug of his drink as he waited for Rowan's reply. Biting back the urge to tell him to back off, Rowan tried not to feel disgust at his liberal over-use of cologne and concentrated instead on giving him the briefest of answers in the vain hope that he would take the hint and leave her alone.

'I moved out of London.'

'Oh. Where to?'

She didn't want to tell him. Having had to fend off the man's unwanted attentions at parties and dinners in the past, she wouldn't put it past him to take it upon himself to pay her a visit. A helpless shudder ran down her spine.

'As far away from London as possible.' The reluctant smile she'd intended barely made an impression on her lips. Matthew seemed to consider her answer for several seconds before pursuing the conversation.

'Still as prickly as a pear, I see.' He grinned, but there was something deeply unpleasant about the outwardly normal gesture. 'You never did like me, did you, Rowan? Always thought you were so much better than me, didn't you?'

It was suddenly clear that he had been drinking heavily. Rowan's stomach clenched tight with distaste. She started to get up off the window-ledge, shocked to her bones when Matthew stretched out a hand to push her back down.

'What do you think you're doing?'

'I think it's about time you and I had a little talk. Set the record straight, as it were.'

'What record? What are you talking about?'

Suddenly she knew she needed to get away from this man. He was right, she didn't like him, and as far as she knew Greg had only tolerated him because he'd to work with the man on occasion.

'Got another man in your life now, pretty little Rowan?'

'That's none of your damn business! Now, please get out of my way; I want to go and find my friends—'

'Greg had someone else in *his* life. Didn't know that, did you?'

About to push past him, Rowan sank back down onto the window-ledge, her brown eyes startled. What the hell was the man rambling on about now?

'You're talking utter nonsense.'

'Am I?'

Matthew's face contorted nastily. A wave of nausea rolled through her and kept her pinned to her seat.

'Didn't know he had a girlfriend and a baby in Turkey, did you?'

Now Rowan really did feel nauseous. If only she'd moved away before he'd started spouting his gibberish. Desperately in need of support, she scanned the room for Jane and Andrew, but they were nowhere to be seen. Probably they'd slipped away to a quiet spot somewhere upstairs where they could be alone for a while. Wasn't that what she would have done if she'd been here with the man she loved?

Suddenly frightened, she pushed to her feet, determined to show Matthew that it wasn't so easy to intimidate her as he imagined. But when she met him eye to eye and his hand snaked out and curved possessively around her bare arm, she found herself curiously unable to move. 'Let me go.' Her voice didn't sound like her own over the thickness in her throat.

'Her name's Anya and her baby son's called Gregory. Gregory *junior*. Naturally, after his father. If you don't believe me, why not ask Dave Madsen or Paul Rutherford? They're his best mates. They know. They were always a little clique, those three. Always kept me on the outskirts of whatever was going on. "Make the tea, Matt." "Bring the extra camera…" "Go and talk to the manager and see if you can get us a better room, Matt." But I was smarter than they thought. I put two and two together when Greg and Paul kept making stopovers in Turkey on the way home. And one night, when Paul had had a bit too much to drink, I wangled the truth out of him. Of course, he made me swear on my mother's grave that I'd never tell a soul, but then I never could keep a secret. Not when it gives me such undeniable pleasure to reveal it.'

'You're sick.' Jerking her arm free, Rowan pushed her way through the throng of people talking and dancing and headed almost frantically to the door. Weaving her way through a maze of stairs and corridors, she finally found herself in the cool lantern-lit garden, the scent of azaleas and early blooms wafting seductively round her senses. Leaning against a granite wall, goose-pimples dotting her skin, she took a few deep gulps of air before rubbing her fingers against her throbbing temple. The man was mad, surely? Deranged, almost. What had possessed him to come up with such an outrageous lie? But even as her brain fought against his perfidy, her heart was thudding so heavily in her chest that Rowan suddenly felt quite unwell.

Greg would never have betrayed her like that. Not in a million years... OK, so they might have spent a good deal of time apart because of the nature of his work, but she'd trusted him absolutely. 'Solid, dependable Greg.' Wasn't that what all her friends had used to say? And not without a tinge of envy. Now, as her mind automatically remembered all the delayed arrivals home, sometimes by as long as a week or more—'because something unexpected had come up'—she tried to shut off her horrible little suspicions, telling herself that she should remember that Matthew Napier was only being vindictive because he'd been jealous of Greg's popularity and knew of Rowan's own aversion to his company. *Oh, God...* She wished she'd never come to this stupid party. Oh, why hadn't she just gone with her instincts and stayed home with Evan?

But 'home' was one thing and Evan another. The two weren't really connected at all. He was her neighbour, that was all, and a temporary one at that. And it wasn't as though they were close. He tolerated her, nothing more. Pushing disconsolately away from the wall, she ran her fingers desperately through her softly tousled hair, a course of action forming in her mind—vague, indistinct, but motivating enough to shake her out of her painful reverie.

'Rowan! Are you all right? Cathy and Linda said they saw you run out here as though you were upset. What's wrong? What's happened?'

Jane, sweet and concerned—was stroking her arm, staring back at her, with Andrew hot on her heels, looking equally anxious. Rowan released a ragged breath, willing herself not to break down in front of them. Later, when she was home again, she could give vent to her hurt, anger and shock.

'I suddenly don't feel terribly well. Would you mind if I went home?'

'Of course not. I'll drive you back to the flat myself and you can crash out to your heart's content.'

'I mean home to Pembrokeshire.'

Jane stared at her as if she was mad. 'Tonight? Driving all that way? You must be joking! Do you think I'd let you go when you've just told me you're not feeling well?'

'I'll be fine once I'm in the car and driving. It—it relaxes me.' Which wasn't entirely a lie. At least in her car, driving through the night, she would be alone with her thoughts and maybe able to think things through more clearly.

'I don't think that's a good idea, Rowan, if you don't mind me saying, love.' Putting his hand on her arm, Andrew smiled down at her as though she were a little child, not capable of knowing what was best for her. Suddenly it was all too much for Rowan and she knew a profoundly urgent need to escape. From the noise, the people, the music, from well-intentioned friends who took it upon themselves to act in her best interests.

'Please, Jane! If you don't want to drive me back to the flat to get my things, I'll phone a cab.'

Jane relented, as Rowan had known she would. 'If it's that important to you that you drive back to Pembrokeshire tonight, of course I'll take you back to the flat to get your things. As long as you assure me you're going to be all right. Ring me and leave a message on the Ansaphone as soon as you get back home, will you?'

'Thanks, Jane.' Giving her friend a brief, fierce hug, Rowan turned and walked ahead of her up the steps leading back into the house.

CHAPTER SEVEN

TURNING over onto his side in his sleep, Evan could have sworn he heard the slamming of a door. He squinted at the small chrome alarm clock beside the bed, and registered seven a.m. Convinced he must have imagined the sound, he told himself he would have a lie-in, in deference to Sunday, then deliberately shut his eyes and went back to sleep.

Later, when he'd showered and dressed, he was on his way downstairs to the kitchen, intent on some breakfast, when instinct made him open his front door and glance outside. As the sharply cold air stole the breath from his lungs and made him shiver, he considered Rowan's car parked outside her front gate with a little throb of alarm. What was she doing back so soon? The woman must have driven through the night to make it back at this hour of the morning. His brain obligingly registered the earlier sound of a door slamming and he cursed himself for ignoring it. All thoughts of breakfast suddenly banished, he shoved his feet into the well-used pair of trainers by the door, grabbed his black hooded jacket from the wooden coat peg, then covered the distance between his cottage and hers in less than a minute.

If she was sleeping then it was just too bad. Evan fully intended on waking her up if he had to, to find out just what the hell was going on. She'd told him she was staying in London for the weekend, so obviously something had come up to make her change her plans. He remembered the peculiar sense of foreboding he'd had when Rowan had told him she was going, and swore to himself to pay more attention to such feelings in the future. Raising the heavy iron door knocker, he banged it loudly twice, the harsh sound ripping through the early-morning stillness, sending a flock of seagulls screeching into the air; uneasiness lined his stomach like lead.

She couldn't have been sleeping because she was still wearing her coat, he saw. Staring at her pale, unhappy face, the huge dark eyes underlined with smudges of grey and blue, Evan experienced a deep jolt of concern as she gazed back at him.

'Rowan...why are you back so early?'

For answer, she stepped back to allow him entry, then turned and made her way silently into her almost emptied living-room. She'd taken the dust sheet off the sofa beneath the window and there was a half-drunk mug of coffee congealing on the newly sanded floorboards beside it.

'I... Parties aren't really my thing.' Sounding as though she was in some kind of trance, Rowan shrugged half-heartedly and tried to summon a smile.

Evan tried to figure out why she was still apparently in her party frock—a pretty silk dress with intertwined rosebuds on a cream background, an item of clothing that gave her an undeniable air of delicacy and vulnerability. His hands curled into fists down by his sides.

'Something happened.' Moving towards her, he

halted mid-stride when she flinched as though struck. His concern doubled. 'What the hell happened, Rowan?'

'I'm forgetting my manners. Can I get you a cup of tea? Coffee? Anything at all?'

'Stop it! Why are you back from London so soon?' Green eyes flashing his impatience, Evan had to physically restrain himself from going to her and shaking the answer from her, because by now not knowing was putting the fear of God into him.

'You're right.' Her chin wobbled slightly and her teeth came down to clamp her vulnerable bottom lip. 'Something did happen.'

'Take your time; tell me about it.'

'I don't want to burden you with my sordid little tale… Go home, Evan. Just forget about it, will you?'

He wanted to tell her he was her friend—that he would do anything in his power to help if he could. But did he have the right when he had done everything to discourage such a friendship between them? He didn't even stop to wonder at the fact his feelings of protectiveness were strong, bordering on passionate. All he knew was an urgent desire to bring hope and optimism back to her pretty face again. But what was this sordid little tale she didn't want to burden him with? What the hell had happened when she'd gone to London?

'Nothing connected with you could possibly be sordid, sweetheart.'

Her dark eyes stared back at him in obvious distress. 'That's where you're wrong.' She started to pace the floor, the heels of her strappy gold sandals making little tapping noises against the bare floor-boards. 'It turns out that my husband, Greg, had a girlfriend and a son somewhere else while he was married to me. Turkey, to be precise. The woman's name is Anya and she is—was a schoolteacher.'

It took a couple of seconds for the full impact of her words to sink in. When it did, Evan's brain absorbed the shock with a chill that turned the blood in his veins to ice. If he could have turned back the clock and acted on that odd little sense of apprehension he'd had when she'd said she was going to London he would have. Anything to prevent this dreadful, hurtful turn of events. She'd idolised her husband. Evan had seen it in her eyes, heard it in her voice when she'd spoken about him. Being bitterly acquainted with betrayal himself, it was easy to guess what kind of emotions she was going through right now. *Torment* hardly began to describe it, but *torture* came close...

'How do you know? Who told you this?'

'Someone at the party who had worked with Greg. I never liked the man, and at first I thought—I thought he was just out to make mischief because I rebuffed his advances—'

'Advances? Did he try something on you at the party?' Unbeknown to him, Evan's jaw had clenched hard at the very thought, his green eyes turning mercurially dark. Rowan shook her head dully.

'No. I didn't give him the chance.'

'How do you know that what he told you was true?'

'As soon as I got back home this morning I rang one of Greg's best friends. Paul also worked closely with him. He didn't want to tell me, but when I insisted on knowing the truth he finally confessed. It seems that the woman lost her job when she fell pregnant with—with Greg's baby. He was supporting her as well as us. It's such a mess, Evan! What shall I do? She relied on Greg. How is she managing without his help? I'd hate to think of the baby suffering in—in any way.'

Stunned, Evan just stared at her. The man she'd married had betrayed her in the worst possible way and there she stood—worrying about how his girlfriend was going to manage financially. He hadn't wanted to be her friend in the beginning, but Rowan was a good person. The kind of woman who made you feel like a better person for knowing her. As different from Rebecca, his ex-wife, as the moon was from the sun. And Evan knew she would need her friends around her now her world had come crashing down around her ears for a second time.

'I don't think now's the time to be fretting about how your husband's girlfriend is getting by, do you? You've had a dreadful shock. You need time to get over that first,' he said wisely.

Her shoulders crumpled beneath her long black coat. By the time her head dropped and huge, racking sobs shuddered through her slender frame, Evan had crossed the room in an instant and impelled her gently into his arms.

'Rowan, Rowan…' Cupping the back of her head with his hand, he absorbed the sensation of her small, curvy body pressed intimately into his with all the shock of being swept up into the eye of a hurricane. For a moment his stunned response simply staggered him. Then when he began to absorb the hungry, sensual demand coursing through his blood, his fingers slid helplessly through the impossibly soft strands of her hair, the sensation of her tears against his clothing making his iron resolve not to get involved crumble like dead autumn leaves.

'How could he?' Hiccuping, Rowan raised her face to his, her mascara-caked tears slipping down her cheeks, like a hurt child. Slowly Evan shook his head. He had no right to want her so badly when she was clearly distraught, but, God help him, he did. As he gently stroked her hair back from her forehead, his brows drew together in genuine bewilderment. 'I don't know, sweetheart.'

'He's such a bastard! How could he do this to me? How could he?' Her tears fell fast and furious from her shimmering brown eyes, demanding answers Evan knew she would probably never discover. Her husband was dead. Nothing was going to change that irrefutable fact.

'I loved him!' She tore out of his embrace, staring at him as if nothing in the world would ever make sense again. In some crazy way, Evan mourned the loss of her innocence. People like Rowan didn't deserve to be betrayed. He, on the other hand… Well. Perhaps he hadn't always been as generous or as understanding as he would have liked. Maybe Rebecca had had good cause to treat him the way she had? Brushing the uncomfortable thought away, Evan stared back at Rowan with sudden, aching need consuming him.

'Say something, goddammit!' Fury was eating her up with a vengeance. As Rowan glared at the tall, handsome man regarding her so coolly in the centre of her living-room, his implacable expression completely excluding her from whatever was going on right now in his mind, she wanted to lash out and hurt somebody. 'Don't you know how much I'm hurting? Are you so bloody inhuman you don't have any conception about how I feel? You with your arrogant glances and easy put-downs! Mocking me because I supposedly had the "perfect" marriage. Well, it's not so bloody perfect now, is it? I hate you, d'you know that? I hate you!' Hardly knowing what she was saying, Rowan started to cry again. When Evan suddenly closed the distance between them and hauled her hard against his chest, she gulped, her dark gaze colliding with blazing green in a torrent of wild emotion.

'Hit me.'

'What?' Her heart started to race.

'I'm him. I'm Greg—the bastard who two-timed you with another woman. Who fathered a child with her... I'm him. Hit me, Rowan. Get rid of some of that anger on me.'

'No.' She tried to wrench her arms free but Evan held her tight, his face very close to hers, so close that she could see every ridiculously long eyelash and each tiny groove fanning out from his incredible eyes.

'I betrayed you. I said I loved you, but I lied, Rowan. I lied…'

'No. Please…' Her voice was a whimper. Her heart hurt so much she thought she would die from the pain.

'Can't you see the truth when it's right in front of you? You weren't enough woman for me, Rowan… I had to seek my pleasure elsewhere…'

'Bastard!'

Like a flash-flood, rage rose up inside her and made her shake. With almost superhuman strength she wrenched herself free and started to pummel Evan's chest with her fists, her words pouring out in a torrent of hurt and anger and fury. 'I hate you! I trusted you, I loved you and you let me down! I'll never forgive you! Never, never, never!'

Her hands hurt. Hitting Evan was like coming into contact with pure, cold, intractable steel, yet not once did he even flinch at the blows that kept raining down on him. Finally, when she was too weak, too distraught, too spent to care, Rowan sank against him, weeping afresh into his T-shirt. When his hands eased her coat from her shoulders and let it fall to the floor, Rowan kept her face pressed close into his chest, breathing in the intoxicating scent of the man: soap, heat, and…*sex*. In a mixture of wonder and curiosity, she raised her head to look up at him. What she saw there should have made her feet hit the ground running. She was destroyed. The man she had loved had led a secret double life with another woman, and her whole past with him now appeared like some terrible illusion, with Rowan as the casu-

alty. His betrayal had gone straight to the core of her
femininity and womanhood, leaving her sense of herself as a desirable woman annihilated. Right now she
needed something to take the rawness out of that
dreadful hurt. Right now she would take whatever
Evan Cameron was offering and regret nothing af-
terwards. Not one damn thing…

'Yes.' Sliding her arms up around his neck, she
emphatically answered the silent question simmering
in his compelling green glance. 'Yes.' Her voice di-
minished to a whisper, a mere husk of her normal
volume as she saw his mouth descend slowly onto
hers.

His taste exploded on her senses. Suddenly they
were devouring each other, kissing with fury and
passion, pain and lost hope, finding solace in the rawness of desire, too hungry to properly undress, too
eager to explore each other slowly with finesse and
sensuality. Instead they would answer their bodies'
urgency with this deeply primal heat and ask no un-
tidy questions. Not now…maybe not ever.

Finding herself somehow on the sofa, Rowan
helped Evan drag her tights and underwear down her
legs, kicking off her shoes as he hastily eased the
slim gold straps over her heels. Then she lay back
against the soft, plump cushions as he undid his black
leather belt and straddled her. For a moment it looked
as if he might say something, but then he seemed to
change his mind and he claimed her mouth in a hard,
consuming kiss instead. When she finally had a
chance to breathe, Rowan's limbs seemed devoid of
all strength, seized as they were by a deeply delicious

trembling that wouldn't be stilled. Making husky little pleas of longing into the side of Evan's neck, her arm sliding across his back, she shamelessly urged him down against her. He needed no second bidding. In an instant, he'd unzipped his jeans and peeled off his T-shirt. Rowan's hungry eyes drank their greedy fill of the sight of his wide, muscular chest and hard, flat stomach with abdominal muscles ridged like finely honed steel, and she sucked in a suddenly frightened breath. She let it go on a gasp as Evan slid his hand sensuously up the inside of her thigh and commandingly urged her legs apart.

Everything about the woman was driving him wild. Her scent took him prisoner, infiltrating his blood so that he felt drugged with it, crazy for her. Her huge dark eyes with their wonder and their raw, undisguised need turned him on like nothing he'd ever imagined. But that was until his hands settled on her body, her slender, silky curves beneath the wispy scrap of material that passed for her dress arousing him to fever-pitch. Self-control at the point of no return, Evan slid his fingers gently into the soft triangle of golden hair at the juncture of her thighs, pleasure throbbing through him at the sensation of her hot, sweet moistness. She was small, but he never doubted for a moment that he couldn't love her to the hilt. As he withdrew his fingers to replace them with his erection, Rowan moaned deeply and moved her hips towards him. From then on, Evan was lost. There wasn't a single place on his body that he didn't ache for her. He was deluged with sensation. As he filled her with a deep, slow thrust, he thought he would explode with the sheer, rapturous gratification of it and, bending his head, he captured her lips with his mouth, greedy to enhance their sensual coupling with all the tastes that made her uniquely Rowan.

The man delivered everything his body promised. As she raised her hips again, to accommodate him more deeply, Rowan's eyes closed to fully experience the profound joy of feeling his sex inside her. Had she ever known this much gratification with Greg? Her connection with Evan seemed so irrevocable…somehow inevitable, as if they were made to be together like this. Had he felt that too, from the beginning? When his fingers closed around her breast, squeezing and stroking her nipple beneath the clothing that covered it until she thought she would go mad if she didn't feel his mouth there, he seemed to pick up on her need almost by osmosis. Words were unnecessary. Moving deeply inside her, he shoved aside the material of her dress, hearing the material rip but paying no mind to it, then claimed first one softly swollen nipple, then the other, cupping and stroking her breasts as though he couldn't get enough of the feel of her soft, satin flesh. In contrast, his own body was hard and heavy, slick-muscled and beautiful, thought Rowan…a male portrait come to life…

'Ohhh…' Rowan's dark eyes glazed as a new feeling built and grew inside her, then spilled over into ecstasy as hotly velvet waves convulsed unstoppably through her. As he thrust deeper inside her, Evan's gaze was frighteningly concentrated while he watched her come apart in his arms, then followed with his own shuddering completion. Blinking back the hot salt tears that suddenly sprang to her eyes, Rowan stared up into that unfathomable green gaze of his and knew she had lost a part of herself for ever. The old Rowan was gone. With Greg's betrayal there was simply nothing left of the girl she had been, and she knew a deep, piercing sadness at the loss.

'I hate you,' she whispered.

'Yeah.' Evan's smile was sensuous and slow and more knowing than she cared to admit. 'I know…'

She must have rubbed her skin raw by now to wash away the taint of his touch, Evan thought savagely as he waited in her empty front room for her to emerge from the bathroom. But even though the idea had the power to wound him, he believed he understood it. Her trust had been ripped away by her husband's betrayal. Crushed underfoot like something soiled. And now Evan had compounded the feeling by making love to her…though how either of them could have prevented their passionate joining, he didn't rightly know. Something far more powerful and profound than mere desire had been guiding them, inevitably urging them together as sure as night followed day.

Glancing round the empty room, Evan immediately hated the idea of Rowan staying in the house alone for the rest of the day. She was hurting and sad, and in his opinion shouldn't be left to brood. He would suggest an outing: a long, exhilarating walk on the beach, or a hike through the countryside, perhaps? It wouldn't solve anything but he was damn sure it would make her feel better. Evan was intimately acquainted with the benefits of exercise on the mind as well as the body. He knew he'd overdone things in the past, but he'd learned from his mistakes and wouldn't ever let himself get so depleted again. Miraculously, he hadn't had the shakes for a couple of mornings now. Perhaps his own recovery wasn't as far away as he had first imagined?

The sound of the bathroom door opening and shutting again with a decisive thunk suddenly commandeered his full attention.

Dressed in jeans and a baggy checked shirt about two sizes too big, her face pink and scrubbed clean of make-up from her shower, Rowan threw Evan an uncertain glance as she entered the room, nervously tucking her soft brown hair behind her ear before speaking.

'Would you—would you like a cup of coffee or something?'

'I'm not leaving you on your own here today. Go put on a sweater or a jacket and we'll go for a walk.'

Rowan stared at the starkly obstinate expression crossing his handsome face, her glance drifting helplessly over his hard, lean biceps exposed by his black T-shirt, feeling the impact of what had just occurred between them anew. Grief and shock had driven her into Evan's arms, but her own free will and desire had kept her there. Did he regret it? Was he right this minute asking himself what had possessed him to make love to her like that? Passionately and without constraint, as if they were really lovers and not just reluctant neighbours who tolerated each other's company now and then? Her stomach roiled at the idea he would harbour regret. Right now she needed to feel wanted…needed, even if it was only in the most basic way. Greg had violated her heart with his unthinkable behaviour. It was bad enough she'd still been in the throes of grief at his untimely death, and now she had to deal with the reality of his betrayal too. A wave of utter despair washed over her.

Evan saw her face whiten suddenly and glimpsed the flash of panic in her wounded eyes. That overwhelming feeling of wanting to protect her that he'd tried so hard not to own rolled through him again. About to walk towards her, he checked himself, stopped, then dropped his hands to his hips. What the hell was the matter with him? He'd sworn to himself that after Rebecca he would avoid involvement with another woman. What was happening to him that he could so easily forget that vow when he was in Rowan Hawkins' company? He'd never, *ever* taken a woman so recklessly or so passionately before. And neither had desire ever overtaken him so urgently—so that all his senses were completely drowned in the raw, elemental need to make her his own, his mind and body driven by the mystifying, primal rhythm of some ancient carnal drumbeat.

'Please don't feel obligated to do anything else for me,' she told him now, her hands rubbing her arms as if to stimulate some much-needed warmth. 'I'll be fine here, honest. God knows, I've got plenty to occupy me. I won't—won't be idle.'

'Obligated?' His tone was rough with disbelief.

'You think what happened between us happened because I felt *obligated*?'

'I don't know.' As she shook her head slowly from side to side, Rowan's hurt glance was forlorn. 'I don't know anything any more, if you want to know the truth. I'm certainly not a good judge of character, so how would I know what your motives are?'

'Get your sweater. I'll wait outside.' His jaw uncompromisingly hard, Evan swept past her out the door.

CHAPTER EIGHT

'I'LL help you do up the house,' he offered as they walked along the wide, deserted beach. It took a couple of moments for his words to permeate the thick soup-like fog in her brain. When they did, Rowan stole a glance at his determined profile beside her, her heart bumping against her ribs when it struck her yet again how handsome he was, how indomitably *male*. A sudden upsurge of need pulsed through her, almost making her stumble. Wrapping her arms around her chest as if to deny it, she winced as a sharp gust of sea air made her eyes sting.

'You don't have to do that.'

'I can do anything I damn well please.' His voice brooked no argument and almost made Rowan cry, because she knew despite his brusque tone he meant well. He was hurting too, she made herself remember. Hurting because the woman he'd loved had thrown that love right back in his face with cruel disregard for his feelings.

'You came down here for a rest…a—a holiday…' Her voice trailed off in the sound of the waves rushing against the shore and she deliberately turned her face away. She could almost sense the scowl on Evan's face. Did it make him feel less of a man somehow if he admitted to normal human requirements like needing rest when you were tired?

Trouble was, he was such a fine physical specimen. She guessed he probably drove himself too hard to keep things that way.

'We'll get the front room sorted out first. You need somewhere comfortable to relax, so that's got to be a priority. You picked out colours and stuff like that yet?'

'I have. I thought—I thought lilac for the walls and soft mauves for the panelling and skirting.' Rowan tried to swallow over the aching lump that was suddenly paralysing her throat. All of this she had been going to do with Greg. Now she didn't even have the consolation of knowing that he'd really wanted any of it in the first place. Had he planned on leaving her one day for the mother of his child in Turkey? Greg had been a father. Something he'd told her he wanted to put off until they were both a little more settled...until he'd worked more normal hours...even though Rowan had been ready to have a child for a long time. All of a sudden, fat tears were spilling from her eyes and tracking down her cheeks and she stopped walking and turned her face out to sea, blinking desperately to force back emotion.

Evan's chest tightened. She looked so lost standing there, her soft brown hair blowing around her pretty face, her slender shoulders hunched. He began to think that maybe he should stay well clear, because what did he know about comforting anybody? It didn't help that when he was around her all he seemed to be able to think about was making love to her, losing himself in her sweetly seductive heat as her soft brown eyes beckoned him in from the cold, reminding him to be a little more human again. His fists clenched down by his sides.

'Want to go back?' he asked gruffly.

'No,' she hiccuped then shook her head.

'Want me to hold you?'

When she didn't reply, Evan moved slowly up behind her and urged her back against his chest. With his arms wrapped round her, her scent making him ache for her anew and her warmth seeping into all the cold places in his body, he sensed her grow less rigid and become more relaxed as she leant against him.

'Thank you, Evan,' she whispered softly.

A rush of something suspiciously warm crowding his chest, Evan rested his chin on the top of her head and simply held her. Right then, he didn't trust himself to say anything.

They'd been painting companionably side by side for a couple of hours now, the radio playing softly from the kitchen, the pervading aroma of new paint filling their nostrils, and practically every minute for Evan had been pure, sweet torture. It stunned him, the strength of this new need in him to hold her in his arms, to protect her, to maybe whisper promises that he knew he couldn't keep. Turning his head to regard her now, he observed the fierce concentration on her lovely profile as she stroked the paintbrush up, down, across the wall, as if the simple, repetitive actions were acting like some sort of buffer, keeping the emotions that threatened to choke her at bay.

'You OK?' he asked, surprising himself with the anxiety threading through his voice.

'I'm fine.' Turning briefly, she rewarded him with a small, fleeting smile that tore at Evan's heart. He knew it was a lie. He knew she felt as if her insides had been ripped out then crudely reassembled to give the appearance of a heart, lungs, organs functioning normally. For two days now she'd been answering his carefully worded enquiries like someone in a trance—someone who'd decided that perhaps life didn't have as much to offer as she'd once believed, after all. His own concerns about his return to fitness, about what he planned to do when he went back to work, about his future—all faded almost into insignificance in the light of what had happened to Rowan. But, other than helping her to decorate the cottage, Evan knew there wasn't much he could offer apart from his friendship. He didn't dare…not when he knew that a more intimate relationship between them could only bring them both more heartache and sorrow.

'Shall I make some tea?' she offered quietly, her paintbrush momentarily stilled.

'It's probably as good a time as any to take a break,' he agreed, laying down his brush on top of the paint tin. He watched Rowan do the same, then stand up and flex her shoulders a little to ease some of the strain that had gathered there.

'Want me to give you a massage?'

'No!' The look in her eyes was completely pan-icked, and Evan felt his stomach churn as if he had a lead weight inside it. 'I mean...thanks for offering but I—I'm fine, really.'

'You going to spend the next few days we're together pretending that we didn't make love?' he asked bluntly.

Rowan considered the question with heart-pounding trepidation. The way he'd phrased it had been so apt, so true to what she actually had intended, that for a moment she wondered if he could somehow read her mind.

'Of course not! I just—I just...' She glanced down at her paint-splattered fingernails and made a futile attempt to try and scrape some of it off.

'You just want to be clear that I know it isn't going to happen again.'

If he knew how much she wanted him...if he even *guessed*... But Rowan knew nothing good could come of such an affair. They'd both been through the mill in their relationships, so why tempt fate? What they had now was good, wasn't it? They'd become friends, despite Evan's initial hostility, and that was something real and positive to hold on to. Much better than a hot sexual fling that would fill them with regret when it ended and make it forever awkward for them to be neighbours when Evan next returned to the cottage.

'I think it's for the best, don't you?' Without waiting for his answer Rowan quickly headed for the kitchen, her spine prickling with heat because she knew that he watched her go.

Cursing ripely under his breath, Evan threw down the rag that he'd wiped his hands on and let himself out of the front door for some fresh air. He breathed deeply as he stood and surveyed the surrounding scenery with little pleasure. For once the backdrop of mountains and rolling green hills failed to bring any kind of ease to his soul. Mountains just reminded him of the climb he'd had to get to the top, and what for? At the end of the day success had been a hollow victory, because who gave a damn except him? And look at the toll it had exacted—he'd almost lost his life.

His mouth a tight, grim line, he forced himself to breathe out the tension that seemed to hold his chest in a vice. Just where the hell was he heading? Was he forever destined to carry this feeling around inside him that something fundamental was missing from his life? He'd once thought that making his business into a success would bring him all the satisfaction he needed, but now he knew differently. If only he could be just as certain about what exactly it was that was missing, he might be able to move towards some kind of goal. He needed aims, direction in life. He'd always been driven—even as a little kid.

'Don't be so competitive,' his mother had often berated him when he'd turn some innocent game with his friends into some kind of war to come out on top. 'Let the other kids have a chance.' Well…having drive was one thing. Damn near killing yourself because you pigheadedly refused to see that you were driving yourself into an early grave was another thing entirely.

Frustrated and angry in equal measures, Evan yawned and stretched, raising his arms high, his

T-shirt riding up past his waist as Rowan came out behind him. She gawked at the unexpected glimpse of smooth-toned flesh, hotly reminded of the feel of that same flesh against hers as he'd made love to her.

'Do you want to come in for your tea?' She shivered as she asked, not from the cold but from the impact of the intense green blaze emanating from Evan's eyes as he turned. Letting his hands drop to his sides, he simply stood and looked at her.

'What?' Nervously she licked her lips.

'Let's go somewhere.'

Her brown eyes widened. 'Where?'

'Anywhere. We can just drive until we feel like stopping, find a nice hotel, have dinner, then stay the night.'

'I—I can't.'

His eyes darkened perceptibly. 'Can't or won't? I don't care what you say, Rowan, I'm not going to let you hang around here and brood. Go on. Pack something pretty to wear and we'll get going.'

'You think that will solve anything?' The idea of going with him was terrifying, but exhilarating too, in spite of the slough of despond she had fallen into since finding out that Greg had betrayed her. Rowan's heart was pumping so crazily against her ribs that she felt almost faint.

Evan grabbed her suddenly and kissed her hard on the mouth. His heat and command chastened her. Just as she sensed herself begin to melt, he abruptly released her and headed down the path with that long-legged stride of his towards the gate. 'Don't be any longer than half an hour!' he called over his shoulder. 'I'll be in the car, waiting.'

They'd stopped somewhere off the beaten track at a cosy little pub with a beamed and weathered interior and rustic dark wooden floors that creaked when walked upon. There was no fire blazing in the huge bricked fireplace, instead there was a pretty arrangement of dried flowers and grasses, and apart from Rowan and Evan the only inhabitants appeared to be two elderly gentlemen playing dominoes, and a nicely dressed middle-aged couple obviously out for the evening. Despite her reservations at accepting Evan's invitation to 'find a nice hotel, have dinner then stay the night', with all the worrying implications that provoked, Rowan was determined to shake off her doubt and melancholy and at least make an attempt to enjoy herself.

'Thanks.' As she watched Evan return from the bar with their drinks, then settle himself on the wooden stool opposite her at the table, Rowan's smile was warm and automatic. The swift onrush of pleasure it provoked in his belly made Evan almost spill his pint of ale.

'You're welcome.'

'I've never been here before, have you?' Glancing around at the dated sepia-toned photographs of the building in bygone days, that decorated the walls, Rowan was reassured by the sense of history and permanence that it evoked. Her own personal history had been dramatically impacted in a way she'd never expected, and permanence of any kind was just a faded dream she'd once had. There'd be no 'permanent' relationship in her future now, because how could she ever give her trust to anyone again? At the same time it struck her that because of circumstances she'd been forced to adopt the same cynical attitude to relationships that Evan had, and the thought pierced her deeply, almost bringing tears to her eyes.

'I've been here a couple of times for Sunday lunch.' Grinning, Evan placed his beer glass carefully down on the cork mat. 'They do the best treacle sponge and custard you could hope to find anywhere.'

'How is it that such a physically fit specimen as yourself can indulge in such calorie-laden puddings and still look so good?'

To Rowan's surprise, Evan's grin quickly faded, to be replaced by a far more sobering expression. 'Don't always believe in the packaging,' he commented. 'I might have been physically fit once upon a time, but I'm not any more.'

'I don't believe that for a second.'

'Why the hell would I lie about it?'

She flinched at the sudden aggression in his tone. Her dark eyes narrowing, Rowan's gaze swept across his handsome, absorbed features and she knew there was something about his life that he wasn't willing to share with her...something that he felt shamed him somehow.

'So...when did you develop this passion you have for puddings?' Deliberately keeping her tone light, she took a sip of her dry white wine, shivering as it slid down her throat.

'Don't.'

'Don't what?' Her chest suddenly tight, Rowan stared.

'Don't pretend it's OK that sometimes I'm like a bear with a sore head but really I'm a nice guy underneath. I'm not. This is as good as it gets, Rowan, so don't get your hopes up.'

Heat seemed to pour into her body from all directions. He was crazy if he thought for even one second that she nursed hopes about a relationship with him! Knowing what she'd just discovered about her husband's infidelity, how could he even imagine she would even want another relationship? Let alone one with him?

'Right now I don't have any hopes of any kind, for your information, because all I'm doing is trying to get through each day intact. So please don't think that I—that I—' She broke off when she saw his mouth settle into a hard, grim line.

'You're a nice woman, Rowan. When enough time has elapsed, and you've started to heal, trust me, there'll be a queue of guys a mile long outside your door waiting to ask you out. You weren't meant to stay single for long, angel. And you've too much goodness in you not to want to share it with someone special.'

'I don't want another relationship. Not now, not ever! What makes you think you have the exclusive right to be so cynical? You're not the only one who was betrayed. If I want to stay alone for the rest of my life then that's my business, and you've no right to imagine you know what's best for me when you clearly don't!'

Evan weathered the storm. He saw her slender shoulders lift, then fall, and her liquid dark eyes shimmer with unshed tears. The need to apologise and protect rose strongly in him again but this time he was ready for it. He couldn't afford to give her any more than he was doing already and he had to make sure she knew that. Very soon he'd be back at work, and she would have to get on with her life without him around to help her pick up the pieces. Stark but true.

'I would never assume to know what was best for anyone, let alone someone who's just been hurt as badly as you, but cynicism just isn't in your make-up, Rowan. Don't make the mistake of adopting it because somehow you think it might help protect you. God only knows what made your husband do what he did, but that doesn't mean that it's going to happen again. I think deep down you know that.'

'And what about you?'

'Me?' He shrugged those big, strong shoulders and gave her a brief smile. 'I have my work. That's the most important thing in my life.'

She wanted to call him a liar, because everyone needed someone, didn't they? But surprise kept her silent, because her own question bore out the truth of what Evan had said earlier. It just wasn't in her make-up to be so cynical. She'd lost both her parents in her teens and had had to make her own way by getting a job and supporting herself right up until she met Greg, so Rowan knew what it was like to be alone and she didn't recommend it. But right now she was too downhearted to pursue this conversation much further.

'Well. Not much longer and you'll be able to get back to it.'

'I'm going to make sure I finish your decorating for you before I go back.'

Biting back 'don't bother,' Rowan murmured, 'That's up to you', then took a hasty gulp of wine that almost made her choke.

Evan's gut clenched hard as if he'd just been kicked.

Her painful silence tore at his conscience as Evan drove. The first part of their outing had been an unmitigated disaster and now, as he negotiated the sharp bends of narrow country roads with the added hazard of a heavy mist starting to fall, he wondered how he could rescue it.

'I don't think this is such a good idea after all.' There, she'd said it. Watching Evan concentrate all his attention on the winding ribbon of grey tarmac ahead, Rowan knew he must be expecting such a comment. How could he not when they'd barely spoken two words between them since they'd left the pub?

'Sweetheart, right now we don't have a choice. We're too far out to get back home in this fog and the hotel is just about another ten minutes away.'

'Fine. Just as long as you know that I've no intention of sharing a room with you.'

To her chagrin, Evan's stern mouth suddenly split into a grin, and Rowan's heart went racing like some wild animal let out of a trap. Watching the utterly competent and confident way he directed their vehicle through potentially treacherous roads in a rapidly descending mist, she couldn't prevent the wave of heat that ebbed through her blood at the thought of sharing a bed with the man. The one time they had made love it had been passionate and urgent, with little thought to linger and take things slowly, but what would a whole night in Evan's arms be like?

'We'll see,' he replied, stealing a brief, amused glance at her indignant profile.

'What does that mean? I've already told you my decision and I'm sticking to it!'

'Protest any more and I might think you really want to spend the night with me.' Keeping his eyes firmly on the road, Evan found himself anticipating their union with renewed longing. He'd been fooling himself if he thought that just one taste of her would ever be enough. She was like honey and chocolate: the more you had, the more you craved.

'I hate you!' Rowan exclaimed with passion.

'Tell me something I don't know,' Evan replied, his jaw firm as he accelerated out of a bend.

CHAPTER NINE

AFTER the shock of the size and grandeur of the country hotel, whose sweeping conifer-lined gravel drive Evan had smoothly pulled in to, Rowan stood in the centre of the suite he had booked and tried not to think of the money just one night was going to cost. What on earth had he been thinking of, bringing her here? It surely had to be one of the most expensive hotels in Wales—if not *the* most expensive.

On their way up to their suite in the lift Evan had silenced her protest with one of his long, slow, impenetrable looks that dared her to argue, so Rowan had pursed her lips, heart pounding and legs trembling, as the lift doors swished open and they stepped out onto a sea of deep plum carpet behind the porter. Now, glancing around her at the deeply opulent furniture, heavy gold drapes and regal-looking prints adorning smooth, ivory-coloured walls, she sucked in her breath and let it out again slowly. Turning back into the room after tipping the porter, Evan briefly scraped his fingers through his thick dark hair, then glanced around him as if the sight that met his eyes was nothing out of the ordinary.

'You shouldn't have done this.' Her voice alarmingly quavery, Rowan fixed him with a nervous stare.

'Why not?' He shrugged as he moved across the room, then dropped down into a striped winged armchair to the side of a marble mantelpiece as if he'd been born to such luxury.

'*I* for one don't want to be bankrupt.'

'I wasn't suggesting we share the cost.' There was a slight chill to his tone that seemed to warn Rowan not to pursue this particular avenue of conversation if she knew what was good for her.

'But Evan, I...' Wringing her hands in front of her red sweater and long print skirt, Rowan wished she didn't feel so seriously agitated about the whole thing, but she couldn't let him get into financial difficulty just for one night in some pompously swanky hotel, could she?

As he leaned forward to rest his elbows on his knees, Evan's green eyes were maddeningly amused. 'Don't tell me you're worried I can't afford it.'

'Can you?'

Right now his bank account was healthier than it had ever been, thanks to two years of dogged hard work and a few well-chosen investments—not to mention the steadily increasing revenue from his fitness outlets. But Evan didn't think it was necessary right then to tell her that.

'If I find myself unable to buy next week's food, you can be sure I'll be knocking on your door for dinner.'

'That's not funny.'

'Where's your sense of humour?' Leaning back into his chair, Evan stretched out his long legs in front of him and relaxed, gratified at last to have the opportunity to survey Rowan at his leisure. If she only knew what that sexy red sweater did for her figure… He could even see the ridiculous appeal of the demure cotton skirt, dainty rosebuds and all. His blood heating, he pushed to his feet and walked towards her.

'It's not too late to tell the desk clerk we've changed our minds…' Her voice died to a whisper as Evan's hands came down on her shoulders and he stole the words out of her mouth with a deliberately provocative little smile.

'*I* haven't changed my mind. Can't we forget about everything else for a few hours and just enjoy what we have right now?'

Tipping up Rowan's chin with warm, gentle fingers, he smiled into her troubled brown eyes. She thought she heard her heart go thump, but it was difficult to know, what with the sudden rush of blood to her head.

'Let's just take our time, then get ready for dinner…what do you say?'

'Good idea. I won't be long.'

Before Evan had the chance to follow through on the long, lingering kiss he had in mind, Rowan slipped out of his arms and fled into the bedroom with her overnight bag.

'There's no…rush,' he said to the empty room as the door shut firmly behind her.

The room was warm, the company distracting—to say the least—and she had drunk a little more wine than was good for her. Now, as Rowan gazed across the beautifully laid dining table at her companion, she knew it was completely pointless to pretend for a second that she wasn't wildly, irrevocably attracted to the man. There wasn't a woman in the hotel who hadn't glanced Evan's way with deep appreciation in her eyes since they'd entered the building. And why shouldn't they, when the man fair took your breath away with his distracting good looks and the way he held himself slightly aloof from everyone else? He'd surprised her by dressing in a tuxedo and matching dark trousers for dinner, and his expensive cologne made disturbing little asides into her senses every time she caught the scent of it. Rowan's stomach turned cartwheels whenever he levelled those coolly implacable green eyes her way.

Like now, as she surveyed him across the rim of her wine glass.

'What are you thinking?' she asked him dreamily, warmth creeping into her limbs and making her tingle.

'I'm thinking that you're a little tipsy.' That compelling, sensual mouth of his quirked up at one corner in a sexy little half-smile. Immediately Rowan put down her glass and pushed a hand guiltily through her hair. The silky brown strands flopped back across her forehead, defying the new arrangement, and hot colour bloomed in her cheeks.

'Are you worried I might show you up?'

'Not at all,' he drawled softly. 'Besides...how could you not draw attention to yourself? You're a beautiful, desirable woman, Rowan. I'm probably the envy of every man in the room.'

It was a pretty compliment, but clearly not true, Rowan thought, feeling pained. There was no doubt

Evan could turn on the charm by the cartload when he had a mind to.

'Then how come, if I'm so beautiful and desirable, my husband found the need to turn to someone else? Hmm? Answer me that if you can.' Because she was upset, she took another generous swig of her wine, wincing slightly as the alcohol hit her stomach.

'You know I can't answer that. Would it help if I told you I think he must have been out of his mind?'

'That's the wine talking.'

Evan's green eyes narrowed as his hand curved deliberately around the stem of his wine glass. 'You're wrong. My glass is still full, see?'

She saw. Biting down on her lip, she stared at the pristine white table linen. 'I want to go and see Paul.'

'Paul?'

'Greg's best friend. The one who told me about the...about the woman in Turkey.'

Straightening in his chair, Evan gave very little away by his expression but his broad shoulders stiffened visibly. 'Do you think that's a good idea?'

'I need to know if she knew about me...if Greg told her he was married. It's driving me slowly crazy not knowing these things. Maybe Paul can tell me why he—why Greg...' Her voice broke and she dashed away an angry tear with the back of her hand.

A muscle ticked in the side of Evan's smooth, recently shaved jaw. He reached across the table to snag her hand. When she tugged it back, he captured her fingers firmly with his and held on tight.

'Stop torturing yourself. Will it really make you feel any better to know the facts? Think about it,

Rowan. What if you find out other things? Things you wished you hadn't learned? Don't buy trouble…that's my advice to you, sweetheart.'

'That's easy for you to say.' Her heart pounding, Rowan snatched her hand away and rubbed it. She heard Evan sigh but refused to believe that he knew best. Look how he had dealt with his own betrayal. He'd become bitter and cynical and was clearly nursing more pain than he cared to admit. He was the last person from whom she should heed advice for the broken-hearted.

'What do you mean?'

'I mean you're hardly in a position to give advice, are you? What your wife did—it's probably been eating you up inside every day since it happened. You loved her and when she betrayed you it hurt bad. Now it's coloured your whole view on life. You don't believe relationships can work or last…do you?'

'For me personally? No…I don't.' Raising his glass to his lips, Evan drank some wine, but it was obvious it gave him little pleasure. 'But we weren't talking about me, were we? I was only trying to prevent you from further hurt…that's all.'

Did he know how impossible that was? Rowan raged against the despair that suddenly washed over her. Not only had Greg made a mockery of her trust and trampled all over her memories of their life together with his betrayal, but she was also now falling for a man who clearly had no intention of pursuing a relationship with her. Not now, not ever. Hot blades slicing into her skin couldn't have done more damage.

'I think I'd like to go back to our room.'

Rising to her feet, she threw down her napkin and attempted to push back her chair. In her haste to get away she lost her balance and fell back onto the chair with an unladylike thump. Evan was beside her in an instant, his tall, imposing figure leaning over her to assist.

'I can manage, thank you. I'm not an invalid!'

'No, sweetheart. But I think the wine has gone to your head a little and—'

'Are you saying I'm drunk?' Her glare was mutinous, her cheeks a rosy, hot pink, and the soft brown hair spilling across her forehead made her resemble a little girl in the middle of a sulk.

Amusement vied with regret as Evan deftly slid his arm around her small waist and helped her to her feet. She had every right to sulk and be angry he thought: she had heartbreak written all over her and there wasn't a damn thing he could do about it. He signalled the waiter, told him to put their bill on his account and guided a no longer protesting Rowan firmly out of the dining room.

Her head hurt and her eyes felt glued together. For several seconds, Rowan assured herself they were two very good reasons why she should stay put in bed. It was only when the luxurious comfort of this particular bed seemed to impinge on her senses that she remembered where she was, and a good reason why she should get up after all. Cautiously opening her eyes, she let out the breath she had been holding with a sigh of relief when she found herself to be alone. Nor was there the slightest sign that Evan had spent the night occupying the ample space next to her in the huge king-sized bed.

All she recalled about last night was that, on returning to their suite after dinner, she had told Evan she was going to lie down because she had a headache. She'd left him in the main room sipping brandy, and on bidding her goodnight he'd treated her to yet another one of those 'butterfly in the stomach' enigmatic looks of his that conveyed very little of what he might be thinking yet made Rowan think feverishly about *sex*...

But they hadn't made love...had they? True, she'd imbibed more alcohol than she normally would have done, but surely she would have remembered if Evan had even given her so much as a goodnight kiss, let alone anything more intimate. His was a touch a woman wouldn't forget in a hurry, and their first passionate encounter was scorched indelibly on her brain for all eternity. Scrambling for her robe at the end of the bed—a much loved 1920s silk kimono she had bought for a steal—she shrugged it on over her underwear and... Wait a minute. She didn't remember stripping off down to her underwear to get into bed. All she remembered was lying on top of the sumptuous gold quilted eiderdown and shutting her eyes. So how had she...?

Tiptoeing across the deep-pile carpet, Rowan sucked in a breath, secured the robe with its red silk tie and opened the door into the other room just the merest crack. Peering out, she located Evan standing at the window, fully dressed in black jeans and sweatshirt, arms folded across that wonderful chest of his, gazing out at the no-doubt imposing view.

Her first instinct was to go to him, wrap her arms around his waist and suggest in her most seductive voice that they go back to bed and forget about breakfast. But only a woman confident of her charms could do such a thing, and right now Rowan's self-confidence was at an all-time low. Betrayal didn't do a hell of a lot for one's esteem, that was for sure. And anyway, why should she assume that Evan would even want her after her behaviour at dinner last night? She'd deliberately been awkward, drunk too much, then to cap it all returned to their suite and gone straight to bed without so much as even thanking the man for taking the trouble to bring her somewhere so beautiful.

'Are you going to stand there all day without saying good morning?'

Evan had sensed her presence the very moment she opened the door. He turned to see her step reluctantly into the room, her hair delightfully mussed from sleep, expression cautious and that curvy little body of hers encased in a very fetching ivory silk kimono. Having undressed her last night and put her to bed, Evan knew that underneath that kimono she had on very little. Two sky-blue scraps of satin and lace that on Rowan's delectable body were enough to end the resolve of even the most hardened celibate.

'How did you...?' Blushing, she moved into the room.

'I'm psychic, didn't I tell you?'

'You're joking, right?'

Remembering the deep sense of foreboding he'd had about Rowan going to that party in London, Evan wasn't so sure.

'Sleep well?'

'About that.' She slipped her hair behind her ear and smiled sheepishly. That smile went straight to a region he was desperately trying to keep out of this conversation. 'I'm sorry I was such poor company last night. I didn't mean to drink quite so much wine and fall asleep so early.'

'No harm done.' *Except maybe to my pride,* Evan thought wryly. 'Was it a comfortable bed?'

To her total embarrassment, Rowan felt her cheeks flame red. 'It was fine, thanks. Where did you sleep?'

He jerked his head towards the maroon velvet cushions of the chaise longue. 'It's surprising how comfortable those things are.'

'I'm sorry.'

'For what?'

'For spoiling your evening. You obviously thought that you—that we—I mean…'

'That I had a little seduction planned?' His green eyes glimmered as they moved over Rowan with no pretence about appreciating the view. 'That I can't deny.'

'Then I'm sorry you were disappointed.'

'Where is it written in stone that seduction is a prerequisite of night-time only?' His voice lowered to a huskier cadence, and Evan moved across the room to stand in front of her.

Faced with those broad, muscular shoulders, that amazing chest and a mouth that promised to take her to heaven and back, Rowan felt her knees quake, and it took some strength of will for her to even reply. 'I don't—I can't treat sex as some kind of recreation, Evan…even if—even if I'm attracted to you. Greg was the first and only man I'd been intimate with until I met you and I can't change the kind of person I am. Do you understand?'

His expression intense, Evan traced the shape of her mouth with his forefinger, regret vying with blazing need in his eyes as he looked at her. 'I'm not asking you to change the kind of woman you are, Rowan, but you can't ask me to pretend that I don't desire you.' His lips quirked a little with wry humour. 'Right now that would be nigh on… impossible.'

Had she ever been presented with this much temptation before? Rowan didn't think so. Yet did she really want to bring more heartache down on her head by getting more deeply involved with Evan? She was already afraid she was starting to care for him too much, and God knew that it was going to hurt when he finally went back to London and his job. Then loneliness would really hit.

'Yes, but you want intimacy without engaging your feelings and I can't not engage mine. If you just want a fling with someone, then I'm afraid it can't be me.'

He fought back the need to curse out loud, because what she'd said was perfectly true. Still, the need to hold her, to love her for even just a little while, was so overwhelming that Evan had to physically put some distance between them so he could think straight.

'So…we go back to being not so friendly neighbours?' The fury in his voice left Rowan in no small doubt as to what he thought about that suggestion.

Smoothing her palms down her long silk robe, she thought she could use some divine guidance right now, because all of a sudden her need to be in his arms and forget about the wisdom of being intimate with him was tearing her up inside.

'You're going back to London soon anyway. You'll immerse yourself in your work…your ''life,'' as I recall…and you'll forget all about me. When you next visit for a holiday maybe I'll bake you one of my pies specially, and we can have a cup of tea together as if nothing ever happened between us at all!' Spinning round on her heel, Rowan was halfway to the bedroom door when she felt herself yanked back to face a furious-looking Evan.

'You're hurting…don't you think I know that? We're both on the rebound, God dammit! You knew right from the start I wasn't into long-term relationships, so why the big, wounded-doe eyes?'

The ache in Rowan's throat felt as if it was going to choke her. Wrenching her arm out of his iron-like grip, she breathed deeply before replying.

Was this what it was like to feel the last vestige of hope for something good smashed to smithereens, with everything going crazy and nothing at all going to plan? She felt as if she'd just been swept down the side of a rocky mountain, the bumps and bruises she collected on the way scarring her for ever.

'I feel sorry for you, you know that? You carry around that precious wounded pride of yours like some kind of badge! Using it to fend off anyone who remotely wants to get close. It must be a very lonely life, Evan, and believe me, I know ''lonely'' inside and out. But don't worry...I finally get the message that all you were interested in was sex with the grateful little widow. I suppose if I were a less sensitive woman I'd be flattered by the attention. After all, you're such a catch, aren't you? Frankly I wouldn't want a relationship with you if you really were the last man left on earth!'

'You talk about me wearing my wounds like a badge? So go find this Paul whatever-his-name is and find out some more stuff about your husband that you don't want to know, then you can go home and live your nice, safe little celibate life, shrivel up inside and grow old!'

'That's a horrible thing to say!' She dipped her head, her dark lashes spiky with tears. 'I thought you were my friend.'

Right then, Evan didn't think it was possible to feel bleaker. But when Rowan glanced at him, all the trust she'd placed in him clearly gone, he honestly felt worse than he had the day he found out that Rebecca had been sleeping with his best friend. And all because he was terrified she wanted something that he knew he couldn't give her.

Disgusted with himself, he turned away to stalk

back to the window. 'Yeah, well, I'm a bastard, so what do you expect?'

'I don't think you're a bastard.' Her voice was soft, all the fight gone. 'I just think you're scared of being hurt. Join the club, Evan...so you're human after all.'

Evan didn't realise he'd been holding his breath until he heard the door shut quietly behind him.

Nobody told her it was possible to have bruises on the inside as well as out, Rowan reflected as she moved the paintbrush back and forth over the same patch on the wall for the third time. She felt deluged—numb, as if crashing rocks had fallen on her head and left her for dead. Since Evan had driven them back from the hotel yesterday morning, there wasn't so much as an inch on her body that didn't ache with regret and longing that things hadn't turned out between them as well as she'd secretly hoped. Because now there was nowhere to hide from the fact that she had been nursing a secret, vain hope that somehow, some way, she and Evan could progress from the tentative, brittle relationship they had to something more deeper and more lasting. But the man didn't want to know, not in the way that she yearned for him to. And now, as well as finding herself a widow and betrayed, she found herself rejected by a man she had seriously grown to care for. If she were paranoid she might start to believe that somebody up there really didn't like her.

There was only one thing she could do under the circumstances. Carry on with her life and forge ahead

with the new start she had envisaged for herself in
the beginning, just after Greg had died. She would
do up the cottage a treat: she would make it a project,
give herself goals to aim for each day, anything to
give her some sort of purpose and shape to her day.
Better still—anything to keep herself from brooding
over every sorry thing that had happened.

But like most things in life it was easier said than
done. Putting down the paintbrush, then pulling the
band from her pony-tail, Rowan shook her glossy
brown hair free and went into the kitchen to put the
kettle on. Helping herself to a biscuit, she took a bite
and almost jumped out of her skin when the doorbell
impinged rudely on her already shattered nerves.

'Can I come in?'

She knew it would be Evan, but finding him standing there in the rain still came as a shock. As she'd
started towards the door she'd warned herself to stay
aloof, be somehow remote, make him see that she
was nobody's fool—least of all his. But all her attempt at bravado flew out of the window when she
saw the bleakness in his haunted green gaze.

'You may as well, now that you're here.' Turning
her back, she edged past the furniture still blocking
the hallway and went straight into the kitchen.

'I see you've made a start on the painting.' He
spoke as if the words were painfully inept—a disguise for something else that he couldn't bear to articulate. Rowan sighed.

'I want my living-room back.' She plugged in the
kettle as she spoke, then set about arranging cups
onto saucers. In all the chaos, a little thing like pretty

bone china helped to remind her there was still beauty in the world. 'I'm tired of living like a refugee in the kitchen.'

There was a rustling sound behind her and she turned to see that Evan had removed his raincoat and was spearing his fingers through his damp hair, looking around him as if he meant to stay. Her pulse raced. So maybe he hadn't come to tell her there was no future in them seeing each other, after all? The tiniest flame of hope flared in her heart.

'Well, I'm here to give a hand,' he informed her gruffly, and before she could reply made his way back out into the living-room. Rowan followed him.

'You don't have to do that. I can manage fine on my own.'

'I've no doubt of that, but it'll be done quicker if both of us do it. Then you can resume normal life again.'

'If only it were that easy.' With a fleeting, unhappy smile, Rowan wrenched her gaze away and returned to the kitchen.

CHAPTER TEN

HE HAD had the shakes again this morning. He'd cursed, then looked into his shaving mirror and seen stark, cold fear in his eyes. Now, as Evan moved the paintbrush up and down the walls in smoothly fluid strokes, he started to feel calmer and more centred. It wasn't so much the painting, he realised. It was simply being with Rowan that made him feel better. There was something about the woman that helped ease the ache in his soul, and even though he knew he had no right to take advantage of her innate goodness, he just couldn't seem to help himself. He knew she was hurting. He knew she was angry. He knew he couldn't ultimately give her what she needed because the last two years had almost broken him, but still he wanted to be near her...for now at least. And if he could make her happy by helping decorate her house, or helping her to get fit, then Evan was more than pleased to comply.

'It's taking shape, isn't it?' Glancing round at the almost completed paintwork, the soft mauve giving a fresh, summery look to the once much darker room, Rowan smiled in pleasure. She was wearing old denim jeans and a baggy blue shirt, her hair was left loose round her shoulders and she wore no make-up. Evan thought she looked ridiculously young and carefree. That was until you gazed into her eyes and saw the hurt that lingered there…some of which he had contributed to, it pained him to admit.

'I was going to start on the doors tonight, if that's OK with you? May as well get it finished.'

'Evan? Why are you doing this? I'd hate to think you felt obligated in any way because of what happened between us.'

Laying the paintbrush across the paint tin, he straightened and wiped his hands carefully on a rag. His gaze was very direct and completely steady when he glanced back at her. 'I don't feel obligated. Let's get that clear once and for all.'

Rowan sank down into the warm, fragrant bath water and sighed deeply as the water lapped over her, stealing the ache from her bones. The bathroom was the one place in the house that seemed like a sanctuary. Before she'd started to tackle any of the other rooms she'd put up pretty lace curtains, decorated the uneven walls with various ceramic plates showing marine life and mermaids, and filled the two narrow pine shelves with a plethora of soaps, foams, bath gels and perfumes. She'd also treated herself to a sumptuous set of deeply luxurious white bath towels, and they were folded neatly over the wooden Victorian bath rail just within reach of the old-fashioned claw-foot bath.

Shutting her eyes, Rowan let her thoughts drift in no particular direction, then tried to rein them in when she found herself concentrating a little too much on Evan, who was still working downstairs.

She'd never known there was such pleasure to be

had in watching a man work. In his black T-shirt, the taut, lean muscles in his arms flexed and moved with every brushstroke, his darkly handsome gaze totally concentrated on the task in hand. Rowan had plenty of opportunity to study and observe. 'Poetry in motion' was her conclusion, after about ten minutes of doing nothing else but sneaking furtive little glances from the kitchen doorway. Everything about him beguiled her—he even managed to elevate the most ordinary of tasks to something beautiful and extraordinary. Had she ever been so fascinated by watching Greg work round the house? She couldn't remember. Right now she could barely remember his face...

Her eyes flew open in sudden panic. People said that happened sometimes after a bereavement, but she hadn't thought it would happen to her. A cold feeling slithered down her spine like day-old porridge and made her shiver. Why should she want to remember his face after what he had done to her? He'd loved someone else, hadn't he? Had a baby with someone else when for so long he'd denied Rowan the chance to be a mother... She was hardly aware that tears were coursing down her face, she was so wrapped up in her pain, and when the door opened quietly behind her then closed again she took a moment or two to scrub them away before turning her head to see Evan standing there.

He'd come to find her to tell her he was finished for the night. He hadn't meant to go right in, but then he'd heard her crying and been compelled to. She'd tied her hair up into some kind of loose ar-

rangement on top of her head, he saw, and little tendrils curled damply around her ears as she stared
back at him with those liquid brown eyes of hers.
Her lashes were long and spiked from her tears and
her mouth looked very soft and damp and pink. As
he stared, his heart pumping a little too fast, the
steamy, scented air from her bath seemed to seep into
Evan's skin and add to the heat that was already
setting him on fire at the sight of her. Desire vibrated
through his blood, demanding, hot and urgent, and
for a moment he couldn't speak.

'You came to tell me you were going home.'
Swallowing down the lump in her throat, Rowan
forced a smile, telling herself not to pay any attention
to the disturbing fact that he had closed the door
behind him. But it was asking the impossible to ignore the fact that he was standing there—all six feet
plus of hard-toned male in tight blue jeans and the
black T-shirt that so lovingly defined the amazing
power in his chest and shoulders—as physically perfect as a girl could imagine.

He didn't move. 'Do you want me to go home?'

It was a loaded question and they both knew it.
But Rowan surmised: what did she have to lose?
She'd already lost pretty much everything she'd be-
lieved in anyway.

'Are you offering me a shoulder to cry on?' she
asked, her voice growing husky.

'Tell me why you're crying.' Somehow Evan
found himself on his haunches beside her bath, his
hand reaching out to finger one of the exquisitely
damp tendrils that clung to her cheek.

'I've had a lot to cry about…wouldn't you say?' A small trickle of perspiration caused by the steam slid down between her breasts. The air between them seemed to grow even thicker. Evan was gazing at her as if she had the power to save his soul, and something in Rowan shifted and settled. Somehow she found herself smiling. Tears and smiles…right now they were hard to separate. She was on an emotional roller coaster that didn't seem to have any intention of stopping. Reaching out, she pushed away a lock of ebony-coloured hair from his forehead, her heart swelling with tenderness at the deep ridges she found there etched into the otherwise smooth skin. Up close his amazing eyes were myriad shades of green and his black lashes unbelievably long and lustrous. 'Stay, Evan… I want you to stay.'

For answer he trailed his fingers in the bubbles of her bath water, his thoughts masked for a moment, as if the steel bars he mentally erected between action and feeling were firmly in place again. Then he smiled, making his whole countenance change, and Rowan let out the breath she hadn't been aware she'd been holding and smiled too.

'Is there room for two in there?' he asked.

Heart thudding against her ribs, Rowan nodded slowly. It was hard to tear her hungry eyes away from him as Evan stripped down to his boxer shorts. The man was mesmerising—his torso beautifully muscled and lean, his shoulders wide and his legs long and dusted with fine dark hairs. When he finally removed his shorts she discovered another area that was equally beautiful and impressive. Drawing up her knees, Rowan waited dry-mouthed for him to settle in the water opposite her, his limbs brushing intimately against hers as the bubbles decorated his skin with delicate white foam.

'Hmm…feels good,' he breathed.

'I expect you're aching from your…from all your hard work.'

'Darling, I'm aching…but not from working hard. Come here.' Before she could gather her scattered wits, Rowan felt her face cradled in his hands while his mouth came down hotly and sweetly on her lips. He took his time, his velvet tongue exploring her intimately as she trembled for him—already the need inside quickly building from 'this is so good' to 'I'm going to die if you don't take me any time soon.'

Under the water Evan's skilful fingers found the soft, hot flesh between her thighs and stroked it. Winding her arms around his neck, Rowan nibbled the side of his bristly jaw, then planted a succession of inflammatory little kisses at the corner of his mouth, at the side of his neck. He groaned, loving the feel of her silky, dusky-pink-tipped breasts pressing into his chest. Right at this moment he didn't have a single doubt that they were meant to be together like this. In fact Evan didn't know when lovemaking had felt so right. His fingers spread her and inserted themselves inside. She was trembling so hard that Evan ached for her doubly, wondering how long he could hold back before he loved her fully the way he longed to. But he wanted to give her the utmost pleasure, so he deliberately took his time, kissing her hotly while his fingers worked their

magic and holding onto her tight when her hips
bucked and her face fell forward against his shoulder
as she whimpered her pleasure.

Wordlessly Evan withdrew his fingers and replaced them with his sex. Raising her hips, Rowan
wrapped her thighs firmly around his waist, taking
him deep inside her. So deep that Evan's heart beat
high and wild and furious in his chest as he pumped
into her, ignoring the fact that the bath water sloshed
frantically around them and finally spilled over the
roll-top edge. Her beautiful brown eyes appeared
dazed and dewy as Evan bent to capture one of her
dusky nipples in his mouth, greedy for the taste of
her as he thrust again and again into her core. Then
in one hot, blinding burst of sensation he found himself spilling into her, emptying himself until he was
spent and drained. Just before, he had registered her
own sudden, wild cry, and Rowan looked stunned as
he withdrew and pulled her into his arms.

Their skin slick with wetness, water spilling everywhere, they held on to each other for long seconds
without speaking. Then, shivering with sudden cold,
Rowan moved her head to glance up into Evan's
eyes. 'Will you stay with me tonight?'

He saw the naked need reflected in the dark, velvet
depths of her gaze and experienced a moment of
panic. He had never meant to get this involved. He
knew he could fool himself he wasn't, but he was.
Right now he was in so deep he was drowning. But
then a feeling of shame swept over Evan, because
Rowan had given him everything and held nothing
back. There wasn't a selfish bone in her body and he

knew it. He'd meant it when he'd told her that her husband must have been out of his mind to have an affair with someone else. So…he would stay the night, and in the morning…in the morning he would tell her the truth about himself. Why he was here, that he had issues of his own that urgently needed addressing before he was whole enough to even think about something like commitment, and Rowan would hopefully understand why their relationship could not progress into something more meaningful…

'I understand if you don't want to.' She'd started to climb out of the bath and, surprised, Evan tugged her down again into the water. He hadn't realised he'd taken so long to reply.

'I want to stay the night. Do you hear me, Rowan? I want to stay.'

Tentatively she placed her hand on his glistening chest and smiled. 'Good. I'm happy now.'

Cupping her lovely face between his hands, Evan grinned back at her. 'Sweetheart, I live to make you happy.'

In the morning, achy and languid from their all-night lovemaking, Rowan slid out of her bed, leaving Evan to sleep. Stealing a helpless glance at one long, muscular arm, flung out across the duvet as he lay on his side, she couldn't suppress the deeply delicious surge of heat that coursed through her blood as she gazed at him. She'd never had a more generous yet demanding lover, and had the faint yet perceptible bruises on her body to prove it. Feeling strangely at peace, she pulled on her robe, sought out her slippers, then made her way quietly downstairs to put some fresh coffee on to brew. By the time she returned to the bedroom, a tray containing coffee and hot croissants in her hands, Evan was sitting up in bed, white pillows plumped up behind him, and a bad-boy smile on his face that made Rowan almost drop their breakfast.

'Where were you? I was hungry.'

She couldn't even begin to pretend she didn't know what he meant. Her blush was as pink as her coral nail polish, and when she put the tray carefully down on the small walnut cabinet at her side of the bed her hands were visibly trembling.

'That's why I went to make us some breakfast.'

'Not for food, you gorgeous, sexy woman. You know damn well what I'm hungry for.' With an impatient scowl he made a grab for her wrist and tugged her across the bed towards him. Rowan's robe fell open as he did so, and when she struggled to sit up the gaping sides revealed her perfect full breasts with their tight pink tips. Evan gazed as though he'd never get enough of just looking at her.

'I'm hungry too,' she said huskily, dragging the sides of her robe deliberately together, 'and I want something to eat or I won't have any energy to do anything.' Scooting to the edge of the bed before he could stop her, Rowan placed a hot, fragrant croissant on a blue china plate and handed it to him. 'How do you take your coffee?' she asked, glancing back over her shoulder.

'Hot and sweet,' came his deliberately taunting reply.

'Some fitness instructor you are!' Rowan quipped back, taking a quick, hungry bite of her croissant before pouring his coffee. When nothing but silence greeted her comment, she turned round fully to regard him. He'd put the plate with the croissant on it to one side on the duvet and was staring in front of him as though in some sort of trance.

'Evan? It was only a joke. I didn't mean to—'

'But you were right. I'm all washed up, Rowan. I drove myself too hard and now I'm all washed up.' Swinging his long, muscular legs over the side of the bed, he reached for his boxers and jeans that he'd thrown across the brass bed-rail last night and yanked them on.

Rowan's stomach churned with dread. If there was a fitter-looking specimen on the planet she would be surprised. But there was something in Evan's voice that told her he was speaking the truth, and that caused her to feel intensely afraid on his behalf.

'What happened? Do you want to talk about it?' she asked softly, her fingers curling apprehensively in the sensuous silk of her robe.

There was a flash of self-loathing in his gaze that riveted her to the spot. 'No, I don't *want* to talk about it, but I guess I owe you the truth after all that's happened between us.' Directing his arms through the sleeves of his shirt, he pulled it down over his head with a bitter scowl. 'When Rebecca left me broke, I gave myself two years to build up my business again. I had bills to pay, and employees who needed wages, and I was damned if I was going to crawl away with my tail between my legs and let everything go to hell because of what that woman had done to me. So I knuckled down and worked as hard as I could. I didn't get to bed till the early hours most nights, and was up again at dawn to exercise and get to work. Slowly but surely I began to claw back everything that I had lost. Thankfully I had built up a loyal clientele, and I had a couple of good employees who supported me through thick and thin. When the business began to thrive again I pushed even harder for it to be a success.' His mouth twisted scathingly. 'You'd be right if you thought I had something to prove. I wanted to prove that no woman on earth was ever going to bring me to my knees again. My endeavours brought me a comfortable living and a business that goes from strength to strength. I could sell it tomorrow and never have to work again. Unfortunately, my efforts also contributed to weakening my immune system. I can't tell you how much my body hurt just walking up a flight of stairs. I couldn't exercise and I couldn't do anything very much except crawl out of bed in the morning and drag myself into work. Then I caught the flu and it damn near killed me.' Shaking his head, he walked to the window, lifted the blue voile curtain and glanced outside, as if his own stark admission had shaken him.

All Rowan's instincts screamed for her to go to him, to put her arms around him and tell him how much she cared. That no matter whether he was as fit as he was before they'd met or not, it made no difference to the way she felt about him. She wanted to help him if she could. They could help each other, couldn't they?

'That's why you came down here to Pembrokeshire…to recuperate?'

'Yeah.' Letting the curtain fall back into place, he turned. 'Then I met you.' There was a heavy, meaningful silence after his statement and Rowan waited with trepidation for what was coming next.

'It makes no difference to me how fit you are, Evan,' she cut in quickly before he could speak. 'All I want is for you to be well…to find pleasure and joy in life again. I'll help you if you'll let me.'

When Evan saw how in earnest she was hope soared for a fragile instant, to be quickly squashed again by a sharp dose of reality. It was a waste of time even to dare to imagine that he and Rowan could have any kind of future together. She wasn't driven, like him. She had no idea what his ambition had meant to him. Not only had he wanted to be the epitome of health and fitness but he'd wanted his business to be the best as well… Then and only then could he allow himself to be remotely satisfied that he'd made a success of his life. With his body weaker after his illness, and his feelings in turmoil about what that ultimately meant for his future, Evan could not allow himself to accept Rowan's concern or help. The woman had been through enough without having his problems to contend with as well.

'When my body is back to full fitness and I can compete with the best of them, then I'll find some pleasure in life again.' Across the room, his green eyes darkened perceptibly as he observed her. 'Not that you haven't given me pleasure, Rowan… You're a warm, generous woman, and no man on earth could resist what you have to offer.'

'But?' Suddenly weary beyond measure, Rowan sank down onto the edge of the bed and waited for him to finish what he'd undoubtedly been going to say. She didn't need to be psychic to know that she wasn't going to like it.

'I can't give you what you're looking for.'

'And that is?' She had a dizzying rush of blood to the head as her throat threatened to close.

'Any kind of commitment. I'm not a good bet for a relationship and I think you know that. Besides…you deserve someone better. Someone whole, for God's sake!'

'You mean someone dependable and likeable and loyal to his friends? Someone like Greg, for instance?'

Evan heard the anguish in her voice and instantly regretted the path the conversation had taken. 'You weren't to know he would act like he did.'

'No.' Rising to her feet, Rowan folded her arms across her chest and gave a tight little smile. 'But if I were yours, Evan…and you were mine…would you have betrayed me like that?'

The question hit him like a tidal wave.

'No,' he said adamantly, his chest in a vice. 'Never.'

Visibly, her slender shoulders dropped and her dark eyes registered pure, undisguised relief. 'That's all I wanted to know. Shall we have our coffee now?'

*   *   *

Her question replayed itself over and over in Evan's mind as he moved the furniture back into Rowan's newly decorated front room. 'If I were yours and you were mine…' Every time he thought about it, it seemed to catch him on the raw. As seductive as the premise was, he had no business entertaining foolish thoughts of turning it into a reality. Once he'd finished doing the jobs around the house he'd promised, he'd decided that he would book a flight out to the Canary Islands, where a friend of his ran a small hotel. He'd soak up some sun for a couple of weeks, in the hope that it would do him good, then return to London and his job.

He'd ease himself back into it, he wouldn't be so ·driven…he couldn't be. There was no doubt he could delegate more. Mike Thompson was an intelligent, astute man—he'd maybe let him steer the ship a bit more. Sighing, Evan paused in his manoeuvring of a sideboard to gather his thoughts. It was no good fooling himself that if he hung around here spending time with Rowan it was going to solve anything. In fact the contrary was probably true. The longer he stayed, the harder it would be to make a clean break when the time came. The woman had been hurt enough. Evan didn't want to hurt her any more.

She appeared at the front-room door just minutes later, dressed in a long, dusky-rose skirt that swished round her booted ankles, a sky-blue top with pearl buttons that dipped a little to give a hint of cleavage and a soft pink suede jacket. Pretty as a picture, she looked, and Evan didn't bother to disguise the frank appreciation in his gaze.

'Where are you off to?' He'd already told her he didn't want her humping furniture around, and had expected her to disappear into the garden to tend her precious new plants.

'I'm going to London. Will you lock up when you've finished? I don't know what time I'll be back tonight.'

Evan sensed the tension gathering behind his brows. 'London? What for?'

'To visit a friend.'

Didn't she know it was impossible for her to tell a lie? She was about as transparent as glass. Pushing up the sleeves of his denim shirt to his elbows, Evan slowly inclined his head. 'You're going to see this Paul guy, aren't you?'

Rowan couldn't deny it. Deliberately avoiding his scrutiny, she ran her glance appreciatively around the room instead. The lilac and mauve walls, the beautifully sanded floor and the newly painted doors had transformed it. It was beginning to look like home again with the furniture moved back in. At least something in her life was going to some sort of plan.

'It's something I have to do. Please don't give me a hard time about it.'

Evan swore. He couldn't help it. He ran his hand frustratedly round the back of his neck. 'How can I give you a hard time when you're already doing that so well yourself? You just can't leave it be, can you?'

Her lip quivered a little. 'I have to know everything.'

'And then what?'

'Then...then hopefully I'll be able to lay the past to rest.'

It was a tall order, and one Evan doubted she'd be able to accomplish. Hadn't he been dogged by the events of his past for the last two years without any relief? It was like getting up every day, getting dressed—then putting on a heavy lead overcoat. That was how much Rebecca's perfidy and betrayal weighed him down.

'Well, I wish you luck, sweetheart, I really do.' Turning away, Evan pushed the heavy oak sideboard flush up against the wall, then dusted his hands.

Rowan stood in the doorway and stared at him, her heart feeling as if it was about to break all over again.

'You don't have much faith in me, do you?'

'I have every faith in you, Rowan. I just wish you'd start being a bit kinder to yourself.'

The look in his green eyes electrified her. She sensed the pull of it deep in her womb and longed to run to him, to wrap her arms around his neck and beg him to take her back to bed, where everything seemed so right and they could shut out the world and its darkness between them. But she was somehow set on this course of finding out the truth, and knew she couldn't rest until she did. Besides which, she also had to come to terms with the fact that soon Evan would be leaving and she would be on her own again.

The thought churned in her stomach and almost made her do that very thing that her desire was begging her to do. Clenching her fists down by her sides, she flushed a little because it was nigh on impossible to look at the man and not want him. 'I will be. After…after this I'm going to concentrate on making this place as beautiful as I can. It will keep me busy. I won't have time to brood…hopefully.' She twisted her hands together but couldn't prevent the anguish that flashed in her troubled brown eyes.

Coming to a decision, Evan rolled his shirtsleeves back down, redid the cuffs, then angled his hard, lean jaw towards her. 'Give me a couple of minutes to grab my jacket and get my car keys and I'll take you to London.'

'No, Evan! I don't need you to come and hold my hand. I'm perfectly capable of—'

'I'm doing it for my own satisfaction,' he interrupted sternly, and stalked from the room.

CHAPTER ELEVEN

PAUL RUTHERFORD had been on edge ever since Rowan and her 'friend' had arrived twenty minutes ago. After wasting at least ten of those minutes taking his time making coffee in the kitchen, Paul paced the floor several times to compose himself before returning to the living-room to face his best friend's widow.

To tell the truth, the big man with the impressive physique and wary green eyes currently occupying the end of the black leather sofa gave him the jitters. There was no doubt the man looked as if he could handle himself, and Paul abhorred violence, especially when it came to a physical threat to himself. But it would surely not come to that, he anxiously assured himself. They were both civilised, modern men... But Paul couldn't help noticing that when it came to the pretty brown-eyed woman sitting next to him, the man had a distinctly proprietorial air that communicated to Paul that he would do whatever it took to prevent her being hurt in any way.

He lifted the mugs of coffee off the tray and put them on place-mats on the low glass table in front of the sofa.

'So...about this woman. This Anya. Did she know Greg had a wife back in London?'

Rowan wondered how her voice could sound so

composed when inside her stomach was churning so badly she almost wanted to be sick. Next to her, she sensed Evan shift in his seat and move a little closer.

Paul lowered himself into a matching leather armchair and leant forward, his forearms resting on his thighs. He looked nervous, Rowan observed, but for once she could find no reason to be sympathetic.

'Greg told her he was married.' Clearing his throat noisily, Paul flashed a particularly apprehensive smile. 'He was going to tell you—' He broke off when he saw the cool glint in Evan's laser-like glance. 'He was going to tell you when he got back from our last trip that he wanted a divorce. I don't know why he didn't. Maybe…maybe he couldn't find the courage? Anyway, please realise this is hard for me too, Rowan. I hated him deceiving you, but he was my best friend. When I saw that he was falling in love with Anya, I couldn't betray him. They seemed…' He glanced down at the floor then back again at a white-faced Rowan. 'They seemed so happy together.'

'I see.' Now Rowan really did feel like being sick. Not only had Greg betrayed her, but apparently he'd been going to leave her for this other woman too. She wanted to shout and rail: what was wrong with her that he could contemplate doing such a thing? But she didn't. 'And what about the baby? How is Anya managing? I understand she lost her job when she fell pregnant.'

Evan glanced at her sharply, but managed to hold his tongue. He understood that she needed to do this, however painful. The least he could do was let her ask the questions she needed to ask.

'It's a struggle for her right now, but she's hoping a friend of hers who also has children will take care of the baby when she finds another job.'

'Well.' Rowan sighed and her hand shook a little as she brushed it through her soft brown hair. 'Perhaps I can help? Greg left me a little money. I could arrange to get a banker's draft drawn up to tide her over for a little while. It seems only fair when she's the mother of his child, don't you think?'

Taken aback, Paul seemed to visibly relax. 'It's very good of you, Rowan, but it's not really your problem, is it?'

'Not my problem that my husband has a baby with another woman then gets killed crossing the road? Then whose problem do you think it is, Paul?'

There was a slight catch in her voice that speared Evan's heart. He covered her trembling hand with his own and gave it a squeeze. Then he looked Paul straight in the eyes and said, 'Have you any idea what she's been through? Can you even begin to imagine the torment?' His temper building, he deliberately held back for Rowan's sake, but Evan was damned if he was going to be all civility and politeness when her heart was breaking all over again. 'Did the man have any conscience at all about what he was doing?'

Paul flushed. 'He said he regretted it, but that he and Rowan...' his pale blue eyes darted briefly to her face '...that he and Rowan had stopped really communicating a long time ago. He told me he wasn't looking for anyone else…it just happened.'

Stopped communicating? Clearly she and Greg had been in very different marriages, if that was the case. As soon as he'd got home from an assignment, Rowan hadn't been able to wait to hear how it had gone, what had happened, who he had spoken to. What had his flight been like? Had he managed to eat decent food? Had he missed her as much as she had missed him? Clearly Greg hadn't been listening to her at all. Obviously his mind had been elsewhere when Rowan had happily chattered away. There was no other conclusion she could reach other than that she simply hadn't been enough woman for her husband—or why would he have fallen in love with somebody else?

Feeling decidedly queasy, she reached for her leather handbag, then stood up. As she turned round to speak to Evan she saw with a shock that he was already towering protectively over her, compassion and something else that she couldn't fathom in his eyes as his gaze swept concernedly across her features.

'I think I'd like to go home now.'

'I'm sorry, Rowan. This is a bloody awful mess, I know.' Scratching his head, Paul appeared shame-faced as he got to his feet.

'I'll organise that draft just as soon as I can. If I send it to you, can you forward it on to Anya? I take it that you're in touch?'

His neck turned beetroot-red. 'Yes. We keep in touch. Only because I was Greg's friend.'

Rowan nodded, forcing a brief smile. 'I understand. I don't suppose we'll meet again, Paul, so take care. I'm sorry we didn't drink the coffee. Bye.'

Evan said nothing as they exited through the door, but the other man's relief was palpable as he threw him a parting glance before pulling the door shut behind them.

'You OK?' Hardly realising it, Evan tightened his hands around the steering wheel as he drove, frustration tensing every muscle because he wasn't free to comfort Rowan in the way he wanted to. Beside him, she looked preoccupied and pale. Her small, slender hands were folded in her lap, and Evan knew to an outsider she would appear the epitome of calm and composure. Ironic when he could only guess at the maelstrom of emotions she must be feeling inside.

'No…not really. But I'll get through it. I'm a survivor, if nothing else.'

The pain in her voice almost undid Evan. Scowling, he accelerated slightly, anxious to get back home, where he could persuade her into his arms and maybe ease some of that pain away.

'What on earth made you offer to send the woman some money? Rutherford was right about one thing—that really *isn't* your problem.'

Frowning, Rowan unfolded her hands and glanced distractedly at her coral-painted fingernails. 'It's not her fault that Greg died. It's not even her fault that he started a relationship with her. People don't choose who they fall in love with. It just…it just happens.'

Her words seemed to reach deeply into a place Evan had long kept shrouded in darkness. Momentarily he released one hand from the steering wheel to massage his chest, but it did nothing to ease the swell of longing that rose up inside him and refused to be tamped.

'Besides…why should the baby suffer because of what's happened?'

'You're too damn nice for your own good, Rowan Hawkins.'

'I can't help the way I am, Evan. No more than you can help the way you are.'

Evan remained silent for the rest of the journey, because right then he didn't trust himself to say a damn thing without getting into deep trouble…the kind of trouble he'd done so well to avoid for the past two years.

Rowan was wondering how she could help Evan. More specifically, how she could convince him to stop all his painful self-recrimination about being somehow less of a man because he wasn't as fit as he'd used to be. In her eyes he would never be less in any way. She was sorry that he'd suffered through illness, but could only thank God that he had pulled through and lived to tell the tale. He was everything she could hope for in a mate, and even if his behaviour suggested that he didn't need anyone close in his life, the qualities of concern and compassion that he had revealed to Rowan on more than one occasion made her believe otherwise.

Ever since they'd returned from London and their

visit to Paul Rutherford, Evan had been particularly mindful of her needs. External ones at least. He'd insisted on helping her put the finishing touches to her living-room by returning pictures and photographs to walls, cleaning windows until they sparkled like crystal, and disappearing off to a local nursery to buy her trays of plants and bulbs for the garden.

Now he was pulling weeds for her out at the back, his thoughts concealed behind an implacable, concentrated expression as he went about the task in the spring sunshine, his lithe, strong physique as eye-catching and as compelling as ever in faded blue jeans and a white T-shirt. Rowan put down the packet of cheese she'd just opened to grate over an omelette, leant on the kitchen sill and sighed softly. Her warm breath made a little cloud on the window-pane and she rubbed it away with her fingers so that she would still have a clear view of Evan.

How long were they going to keep up this charade of outward civility when underneath strong passions and things left unsaid were tearing at them both? As far as Rowan was concerned, she knew that Evan meant more to her than just a neighbour or a friend. She loved him. The thought didn't knock her sideways, because it had been steadily growing inside her over the past few days. She'd nurtured it in her body like a plant about to push through the soil and reach towards the sun. He was convinced he wasn't a good bet for a relationship, and there was probably nothing Rowan could say to change his mind, but still she could love him from afar, couldn't she? Her throat tightened almost unbearably. When he left to go back to London, as he inevitably would soon, she would tell him she would always be there for him if he ever needed a friend, that she would demand nothing more than he felt able to give and that was all. Even if she was dying inside, she couldn't let him know that. The man didn't deserve any more pressure than the ones he was under already.

Evan didn't believe that she could bury the ghosts of her past easily, and God knew the pain of her husband's infidelity and deceit still lingered like the sting of a thousand tiny scores on her heart. But Rowan knew that she would get over it sooner rather than later, because the depth of feeling she had for Evan made her realise that the affection she had had for her husband had been a lukewarm substitute for love in comparison.

Hearing the pan sizzle behind her on the stove, Rowan gave herself a little shake and turned off the gas. Taking a minute to compose herself, she shook her hair free from the pink satin scrunchie that confined it and pressed her palms flat against her skin to cool her burning cheeks. When Evan suddenly appeared from the garden in the kitchen doorway, her heart squeezed with longing at the sight of him and she couldn't prevent the smile that broke free.

'Lunch won't be long... I'm afraid I've been standing here daydreaming.'

'Oh?' He didn't smile back. Instead his intense green eyes shimmered with grave concern. Immediately Rowan knew what he was thinking.

'Not about Greg or any of that,' she said quickly.

'Then what?' Reaching for a tumbler from a glass

cabinet, Evan poured himself some water from the tap as he waited for her reply.

'I was thinking about you, as a matter of fact.' Quickly withdrawing her glance, she looked about for something to occupy her hands. She opened a drawer, pulled out a clean checked tea-towel, then proceeded to dry a mug that was left upturned on the drainer.

'What about me?' One dark eyebrow quirked up towards the lock of sable-dark hair that fell across his forehead, and he leaned into the counter in no apparent hurry to make himself scarce.

Wishing her heart would stop its incessant racing, Rowan rubbed at the mug even more vigorously with the tea-towel. 'I was wondering how you were doing…how you were feeling? You never tell me.'

As Rowan had feared it would, she saw his guard come down immediately—like a portcullis crashing down to protect the inner sanctum of a fortress. Taking a swig of water, he placed his glass down on the counter, then wiped the back of his hand across his mouth. 'I'm fine. Nothing for you to worry about.'

'But I do worry about you, Evan.'

'Then don't.' His mouth twisted a little and he glanced away. 'I'm all grown up, as you can see. I can do all the worrying I need for myself.'

'But…everyone needs someone to care. Nobody should be completely on their own.'

His gaze swung right back to Rowan's heartfelt glance, and if she hadn't already guessed that a tender heart beat beneath that forbidding exterior she would have backed away in fright. 'You may feel like that...understandably considering the circumstances; but *I* don't. I'll be your friend, Rowan, and you can be mine, but if it means you constantly fretting about my welfare then I'll walk out the door right this minute and never look back.'

Cold dread made her speechless for a moment but she stood her ground. 'Why do you always make things so difficult? Are you going to conduct the rest of your life this way? Pushing people away, keeping your distance, not allowing anybody to care or get close?'

'That's my business.' Glaring at her, he moved towards the door.

Sudden fury bubbling up inside her, Rowan was one step behind him when her small hand circled his very strong masculine wrist. 'We made love...' Her lower lip quivered slightly. 'Doesn't that mean anything to you?'

Evan didn't shake off her grip. Instead he replaced it with one of his own on her opposite arm and yanked her hard into his chest. His gaze darkening like an oncoming storm, he stared down into her startled brown eyes, the drift of her scent hitting him somewhere low in his belly, making him want her so badly he didn't know how he stopped himself from dragging her onto the counter and taking her there and then.

'It means we had great sex,' he said harshly. 'But just because I'm physically attracted to you it doesn't mean we've got a relationship made in heaven. I don't believe such things exist. Look at what happened to you; and if that doesn't convince you then look at what happened to me. I'll be your lover, Rowan, but I won't be your happy ever after… That clear?'

A word hovered on her lips—the harsh, detrimental one he had used before to describe himself—but Rowan was too distraught to articulate it. Instead, her teeth came down hard on her lip as she struggled to contain her hurt and dismay.

'I don't want you to be my lover. I don't want you to do anything for me. I'd rather be on my own than waste my time with such a cynical, bitter man as you! Now, if you don't mind letting go of my arm, I've got lunch to prepare.'

He dropped her limb like a hot potato, nodded tersely, then exited the room without saying another word. When Rowan heard the front door slam, she turned her face to the window and gave free rein to the painful sobs that had been trapped in her throat.

He knew it was probably the most cowardly thing he had ever done, but Evan honestly didn't feel able to witness the recrimination and reproach he knew he would see in Rowan's gentle brown eyes. Already he'd hurt her too much with his cruel words and pretended indifference. If he stayed around much longer he would end up hurting her even more and he didn't want that. He'd never wanted that. Pausing for a moment, he thumped his chest to release the harsh breath that had become trapped there. Would the woman ever be able to trust another man again after this?

He stood on the step of his cottage, staring out

unseeingly at the wild, untamed beauty of the
Pembrokeshire hills—his fingers closing around the
paper in his pocket as if it was dynamite. But it was
no good delaying things any longer. He'd made his
decision. It might be one that would be hell for him
to live with, but at least Rowan would have a chance
to take stock and realise that he wasn't the man for
her. He walked across to Rowan's house like the pro-
verbial condemned man, his brow breaking out in a
sweat, his legs as heavy as lead.

Scowling as he pushed the folded-up note into her
letter box, he hurried back down the path, shutting
the gate carefully behind him, scarcely knowing what
he would do if she should appear at the door right
then. He'd probably grab the note right back and history would take a different path from the one he intended. But when Rowan didn't appear Evan resigned himself to the fact that he'd made the right
decision after all—even if it was one he hated. Then,
without looking back, he climbed into his waiting
Range Rover, gunned the engine and drove determinedly away before he did something stupid…like
change his mind.

All the way back to London his chest felt as if it
was clamped in a steel trap that made it difficult to
breathe. Every time he imagined the hurt on her face
as she read his aloof little note he died a thousand
painful deaths, and almost had to pull over onto the
hard shoulder to compose himself. But he wouldn't
look back, he told himself. He wouldn't regret leaving her, because what did he have to offer a gentle,
wounded soul like Rowan? If he stayed it was a cold,

hard fact that he would only end up hurting her even more. She was right. He *was* bitter and cynical. Two years after his divorce, he was still eaten up with anger at Rebecca's treatment of him. How could he even begin to imagine he could have another relationship when he still had so much baggage to contend with from his past? Better let her make a new life for herself sooner rather than later and she wouldn't be able to do that while he was the main presence in her life. He would miss her but it was better this way…

But better for who? Evan wondered bleakly as he automatically switched on the wipers to deal with the rain that was suddenly ricocheting off the windscreen.

Rowan drove home from the doctor's in a daze. The two bags of groceries that she'd lain on the back seat spilled out as she negotiated the twists and turns of the narrow country lanes back to the cottage, but she couldn't have paid them less attention. Her heartbeat was thundering so loudly in her ears that it obliterated the sound of everything else —even the odd passing car that flashed by in the opposite direction.

She was pregnant…eight weeks pregnant with Evan's child. Now, as she stared through the windscreen, tears spilled freely from her eyes and slid hotly down her cheeks. Who would have believed something good—a miracle, even—could come out of something that had hurt her so badly? When Evan had left her that cold little note six weeks ago, saying he was sorry but he needed to make a clean break and get back to his work, she had never felt so desolate or lonely in her life. Suddenly Greg's betrayal and the subsequent truth of their marriage had paled almost into insignificance in comparison.

It was Evan who had her heart…who would always have it, because she couldn't ever be with anyone else now that he'd gone. And now she was going to have a child of her own. A baby they had made together. Whether he liked it or not, there would always be a part of him in her life once the baby came. In spite of her tears, Rowan couldn't help but smile at that. She would be the best mother, she vowed silently, because fate had intervened and given her the much longed-for child she had always fantasised about. God moved in mysterious ways, people said…and as far as Rowan was concerned, they were right.

Later on that evening, as she glanced round the interior of her sunny little cottage, fierce pleasure coursing through her at the sight of every beautifully decorated room, she knew she had come a long way from the shy, trusting girl she had been when she'd been married to Greg. All of a sudden she felt like a grown-up—a woman in charge of her own life, making her own decisions without deferring to a man. The fact that the man she loved wasn't in her life right now wasn't going to bring her to her knees, because even if Evan was adamant he could not commit to a proper relationship with her, she understood his fear and forgave him for it.

Now, noting all the little carefully added personal touches, like books, mirrors, houseplants and prints, lovingly selected to enhance each room's individuality, Rowan made her way slowly upstairs to the bedrooms. The sunny box room with its attractive leaded windows would make the perfect place to put her baby's cot. But for the first couple of months she fully intended to have the infant in the same bedroom as herself, in a beautiful wooden cradle that she would scour the antique shops to find, then restore.

In the middle of her plans, Rowan's heart stalled. She would have to tell Evan about the baby. Oh, she knew already it wouldn't make any difference to his decision about their relationship, but she refused to start off her baby's life with a lie. Lies had played a big part in the desecration of her marriage to Greg— she was adamant that Evan would know the truth about the child they had created together, then it would be up to him whether he wanted to be involved in their lives or not. As she thought about that Rowan leant back against the wall, hugging herself, as if to protect both herself and the baby.

CHAPTER TWELVE

His long legs stuck out in front of him, his feet on the desk, Evan savoured the first quiet moment he'd had all day and briefly shut his eyes. Somewhere in the back of his mind he registered the sound of the aerobics instructor, issuing orders to her class sergeant-major-like as pop music blared out from the music box she always toted with her. It was testimony to his single-mindedness that he was able to blank it out almost completely with thoughts about his plans for the weekend.

He was going to visit Beth and the boys and spend some time with them. Instead of dropping by for five minutes then dashing back to work again he was going to stay around until Sunday, take them all out for lunch at one of London's top hotels, followed by a trip to the cinema for the latest blockbuster action movie that they were all dying to see. Breathing out slowly, Evan continued to keep his eyes closed. His staff knew better than to disturb him when he was taking his now regular twenty-minute afternoon break. He'd instigated the new regime on his return from the Canary Islands, vowing to himself that he would never work himself into the ground again or compromise his health.

He was starting to feel better. Everything was

starting to feel better…except for the fact that he didn't have Rowan in his life any more.

His eyes flew open. Reaching for the cream vellum envelope he'd put in his 'out' tray, he stared at the familiar address on the front for a few seconds before dropping it back down on top of two other letters ready for the post. Swinging his legs off the desk, he stood up in a bid to try and contain the sudden restless wave of energy that was coursing through him. To distract himself he went to the water cooler and poured himself a drink. The knock on the door took him by surprise. Frowning, he turned towards it, ready to tear whoever it was off a strip for disturbing him when they'd been strictly briefed not to.

'I thought I told you I wasn't to be dist—'

'Hello, Evan.'

His heart started to pound at the sight of the woman he'd been so desperately determined not to think about. In a pink summer dress that floated down to her ankles, an array of colourful bangles adorning her wrists, her hair arranged in a loose topknot with golden tendrils floating loose around her ears, she was the epitome of grace and femininity. Somewhere in his chest Evan's breath got trapped. 'Rowan. Somebody should have told me you were here.'

'I should have made an appointment,' she admitted, clutching her square crocheted bag with its bright yellow daisy motif to her chest, 'but I couldn't pluck up the courage. I thought if I was going to do this I just had to come, and not talk myself out of it.'

'Why don't you sit down? Can I get you a drink? You look hot.'

It wasn't how she wanted to look at all, Rowan thought, miserably stroking away the perspiration that had gathered on her brow. She wanted to look cool and sophisticated…she wanted Evan to think her beautiful…she wanted him to regret every single moment he'd been away from her, even if she knew that was about as likely as Third World debt being wiped out tomorrow…

'It's a glorious summer's day out there.' Her smile retreated almost as soon as it appeared, her glance nervous. He was the one who appeared cool. Cool and unruffled and in control, in his black sweats and to-die-for bronze tan; those remote green eyes of his exposing nothing—least of all pleasure in seeing her.

'Yeah,' he said wryly, 'and I'm stuck in here.'

Rowan had been more than a little taken aback when she'd arrived at the state-of-the-art gymnasium, the sumptuous carpets in Reception and the beautiful blonde behind the desk with her slightly haughty glance almost making her want to turn back through the automatic doors and go home again. But she had to do this. For her baby's sake if nothing else…

'So…how have you been keeping?' she asked, a just-discernible tremble in her voice.

The question was full of heartbreak, and Evan wondered how he was ever going to forgive himself for running out on her in such a cowardly fashion, even when at that particular time he'd honestly believed he had no alternative.

'I'm fine,' he said honestly. 'I'm doing much better. How about you?'

Her brown eyes darted away for a moment, scanning the room, her gaze alighting on several framed certificates of merit and fitness qualifications that adorned the wall behind Evan's desk.

'You said in your note that I could contact you if…if I needed anything or if there was an emergency…'

'What's wrong? What's happened?' His voice was like a whiplash and it startled Rowan. Swallowing across the sudden pain in her throat, she clutched her bag against her even tighter.

'I'm pregnant,' she said breathlessly, 'eight weeks, to be exact. I'm going to have your baby, Evan.'

He didn't ask her to repeat what she'd just said because Evan knew instinctively that every word was true. If ever there was a woman incapable of lying then that was Rowan. In terms of decency and honesty she was light-years apart from Rebecca—his ex-wife. Rowan hadn't told him she was pregnant to try and trap him…she'd merely told him the truth, honestly and directly—and, God help him, what was he going to do about it?

'Did you…did you hear what I said?' Moving towards a leather swivel chair, Rowan gave in to a sudden desperate need to sit down, her sunny yellow bag clutched tightly in her lap, her dark gaze apprehensive.

'I heard you.'

At the flat monotone of his voice hope was swept away like debris in the wake of a storm. Her fingers gripped the soft crocheted bag even harder, her nails digging into the material for support. 'I thought you should know. I didn't want any more lies in my life. You can be a part of the baby's life or not…it's up to you. I didn't come to make demands or to pressurise you in any way. Anyway, now you know.'

Because she feared she might break down in front of him, Rowan got hastily to her feet, her chest hurting so badly that suddenly there wasn't enough air to breathe. He didn't care, she realised disconsolately. It didn't make any difference to him whether she was carrying his child or not; he still saw no future in a relationship with her. Better that she'd found that out now than nurse false hopes indefinitely. Now she knew that Evan categorically wasn't interested in either her or the baby, she could press on with her life without him.

Her head began to swim as she started towards the door, and she was unprepared for the shock of his touch as his hand whipped out to possessively encircle her wrist.

Her startled gaze fell into a sea of green and her heart almost thudded right through her chest at the expression she saw there.

'Where do you think you're going?'

'Home. I've parked my car at Jane's and now I'm going to get the tube and go back there. It's a long drive back to Pembrokeshire, and I'll be too tired to face it if I leave it much later.'

'I'm not letting you make that long drive back tonight. You can stay at my flat, then I'll drop you off at Jane's in the morning. OK?'

It wasn't OK. Nothing was OK. Suddenly deathly tired, Rowan tried to extricate her wrist. Evan wasn't having any of it. He held on as if he never intended to let go again. Her brown eyes widened in confusion.

'You've seen a doctor, I take it?' he enquired brusquely.

'You think I'm lying to you?'

A muscle trembled in the side of his tantalisingly smooth, tanned cheek. 'Did I say I thought you were lying? I just wanted to make sure you were being looked after.'

'Why? Because it absolves you of any responsibility?' Heartsick, Rowan stared at his wide, muscular chest in the dark sweatshirt, the colour swimming before her eyes. She felt her chin tipped up again so that she had to face him, her pulse quickening at the piercing glance he gave her in return.

'No. Because I want you and my baby to have the best care... Is that so hard for you to believe?'

'My baby' he'd said. Hope leapt inside her. As fragile as rice paper, but hope just the same.

'You haven't said how you feel about it, so how would I know?'

'I won't pretend it hasn't come as a shock. And we need to do some serious talking, that much I do know.'

'So we'll talk. I don't need to stay at your flat tonight. Perhaps once I get home, and you've had time to think things over, you can ring me and let me know? As I said, I don't want you to feel pressurised. I know you don't want commitment. I just thought it would be good for the child if he or she could see you once in a while…that was all. But if you don't want that, I'll understand.'

'Just like you understood when your husband had an affair and got his girlfriend pregnant? And when his gutless friend told you he'd been planning to leave you for the woman? For God's sake, Rowan! Don't you think it's time you stood up for what's yours?'

The fury blazing in his eyes took her aback. His hand tightened its grip on her wrist, then he let it go abruptly as if disgusted with himself.

'What's mine?' Her lip trembled and she was helpless to prevent it.

' "If you were mine and I were yours" …isn't that what you said?'

'But Evan, I—'

'Oops! Sorry, boss…didn't know you had a visitor.' A tall, athletic-looking young man with cropped dark hair bowled into the room without knocking.

Guiltily, Rowan took several steps away from Evan and went round the desk to examine more closely the impressive array of certificates and diplomas on the wall, but she hardly saw them at all because her concentration was blown to smithereens.

'Can't a man have any privacy round here?' Evan barked, irritably scraping his fingers through his thick black hair.

'Chris has just phoned in sick,' the other man related quickly. 'He's due to take a class in half an hour and I was wondering if you could do it.'

'Fine. What's wrong with him?'

'Thinks he's coming down with the flu.'

'Ring him back and tell him not to worry about getting back until he's properly recovered. Between us we'll cover for him.'

'Thanks, boss.' With a fleeting interested glance in Rowan's direction, the young man quickly exited the room. Hearing Evan exhale slowly behind her, Rowan squared her shoulders before turning round. 'I don't want to be a problem—' she began.

'I never, ever suggested you were a problem, did I?'

'Your note said—'

'Forget the damn note! I took the coward's way out and you know it. You should be furious with me—why aren't you?' Before she could answer him, Evan paced the floor to the other side of the room and back again. He was wound up as tight as a clock and Rowan hardly dared breathe. Right now it seemed that one word or sound out of place could tip the precarious balance between them as easily as a butterfly's wing.

'You have a right to be angry, Rowan. When people treat you badly you have a right to express your disappointment. Don't keep it all inside and let it chip away at your confidence.'

Still she said nothing. A bead of perspiration rolled down her back between her shoulderblades. Although there was a fan whirring in the corner of the room the air was too close, oppressive, even. It made it hard for her to think. Finally, she found her voice. 'And have you resolved all your anger, Evan?'

'What happened between me and Rebecca is

firmly in the past—a time and place I don't intend
to go back to any more if I can help it. What I'm
interested in now is my future.' Raising the slats of
the pale ivory blind at the solitary window, he peered
through it for a few seconds before continuing.
'Mine…and yours.'

The two didn't necessarily go together, Rowan
thought miserably, but when Evan made her the sole
focus of all his attention once more it was hard to
hold his glance, it was so frighteningly intense. Instead she found herself studying the glossy brochures
advertising the gym spilled across his desk, specifically the nubile and very fit-looking young blonde
pounding a treadmill.

An uncertain little smile tugged at her lips. 'You
were going to help me get fit. I suppose it will have
to wait now until after the baby…getting fit, I mean.
It doesn't mean that you have to—'

'Did you hear what I said?'

All of a sudden he was standing in front of her—
a tall, imposing, awesomely fit-looking male with
ebony-black hair and green eyes seductive and dangerous enough to make a mother lock up her daugh-
ter until she was old. Suddenly drenched in heat,
Rowan lifted her gaze to meet that unashamedly bold
glance of his. 'I heard.'

'And do you know what I mean by it?'

'Yes… No… I mean… Stop looking at me like
that! I can't—I can't think when you look at me like
that!' Hot and flustered, Rowan would have moved
away if it hadn't been for the fact that Evan had

taken her bag from her and thrown it on the desk and now had firm hold of both her hands.

'I've missed you, Rowan.' The sincerity in his words made his voice seductively hoarse—like whisky and cigarettes.

Rowan's beleaguered heart soared into the sky. 'I've missed you too, Evan,' she said softly. 'Too much.'

His kiss was gentle at first, almost as if he was afraid to touch her, as if the contact after weeks of separation was too much to bear. He tasted and drank from the honey of her lips in brief, hungry little bursts, but then his hands were cupping her face, as if to anchor her, and his tongue was thrusting into the hot sweetness of her mouth, demanding everything. Desire ignited between them, fervent and rapacious and hot enough to start a serious conflagration.

Sliding her arms around the hard-muscled strength of his torso, with the evidence of Evan's passion pressing hard against her belly, Rowan surrendered to his ardent demand, loving every second of his touch, her senses exploding with the realisation that perhaps he did care for her and the baby after all. The thought sent adrenaline crashing through her like a rapid. Twisting her mouth away from Evan's, she stared up at him, her warm brown gaze anxious and uncertain. She had to know the truth about how he felt.

She had to know it once and for all. Passion was one thing, but Rowan knew that it wouldn't sustain her through the long years that hopefully lay ahead.

Without love, passion was like a sumptuous banquet left to grow cold.

'About the baby. I need to know how you feel, Evan. I've had sleepless nights wondering how you would take the news…whether you would even want anything to do with me again. Your note was so…so cold.' A shadow came over her gaze and Evan brought his hands down to the softly flaring curve of her hips in her filmy pink summer dress and held her there.

'Aren't I showing you how I feel?' One corner of his mouth kicked up in a sexy little grin.

Rowan bit down on her lip. 'That's not what I meant. Would you have got in touch with me again if I hadn't come here today?'

Turning his back momentarily, Evan reached into his 'out' tray for the cream vellum envelope he'd dropped on top. Without preamble he gave it to Rowan. 'I've been meaning to send this for the past month, but I worried that if I sent it you'd merely tear it up and throw it away. Finally today I got up the courage to go ahead and send it.'

Extracting the beautiful gilt-edged card from its crisp envelope, Rowan briefly admired the study of a woman standing amongst the flowers in her garden before opening it carefully to read the words inside. It read: *You have my heart and always will. Evan.*

'There's only one woman who I want to be the mother of my children, Rowan…and that's you. That make it any clearer for you?'

Words deserted her.

As Evan absorbed the beauty of her face, it finally

hit him like a sledgehammer just how much this wonderful, gorgeous, courageous woman meant to him. Although his sojourn in the Canary Islands had helped to restore his health and fitness, mentally he had been in torment since he'd walked out on Rowan. As the days and weeks had gone by, and he'd finally returned to work, he'd found it harder and harder to live with himself because of what he had done. But the most telling sign of all that he needed her in his life, for now and for ever, was the fact that he missed her morning, noon and night. No longer were his thoughts saturated with memories of Rebecca's perfidy or betrayal, because at last he had let go of the anger and hatred that had been chewing him up inside. Now instead his thoughts were full of images and memories of Rowan—and the fact that she was now in his arms, having told him she was pregnant with his child, was like a miracle. A miracle he hardly deserved.

'I'm sorry I walked out on you like I did. I didn't mean to be cruel. That note…' His handsome brow creased as if he despised even the mention of it. 'I had all these feelings for you, and frankly they scared me senseless. You'd already been hurt more than I could bear, and I was terrified that I would cause you more pain by not being able to commit. Can you understand that?'

'I can understand it perfectly.' Her smile was brighter and more dazzling than the sun beaming down outside on London's hot pavements. 'Lucky for you I'm such an understanding, forgiving soul.'

'You're an angel.' Drawing her close into his

chest, Evan shook his head in wonder as he took in
her soft brown hair, escaping in clouds of silk around
her ears, and her dark, melting eyes as they gazed
up at him with a warmth so profound it had the
power to make him her slave for life.

Rowan laughed softly. 'Oh, I wouldn't go that far.
I can be as cranky and moody as the next hormonal
woman, so be warned!'

'I love you.' He kissed her once, twice, three
times, before raising his head to study her once more.
'Do you think you'd be willing to take another
chance on wedlock and marry me?'

Suddenly shy, because her heart was too full for
her to speak, Rowan managed the faintest of nods.

'Can I take that as a yes?' Evan prompted, a smile
tugging at his gorgeous mouth.

Laying her palm against his chest just above his
heart, Rowan let all the love she felt for this once
angry, taciturn, wounded man radiate like a sunburst
from her eyes.

'I want you to know that I'm marrying you because I love you, Evan...not just because of the
baby. You're a good man, even if you sometimes
doubt it, and I would trust you with my life.'

'And I guess I've got that ridiculous straw hat of
yours to thank for introducing us. We might never
have spoken if it weren't for that.'

'Hmm...there was always my creaking gate, remember? The one you insisted on fixing even though
I didn't want you to!'

'Perhaps there were other forces at work in our
case.' In a mood for conciliation, Evan tweaked her

earlobe affectionately then, bending his head, got reacquainted with her lips as only a man in love could.

Rowan walked out into the garden. Hugging her arms across her chest in her shell-pink cardigan, she marvelled at how here, in this wild, sometimes inhospitable part of the country, the weather could change so suddenly. The day had been sultry and almost unbearably hot, but now as Rowan looked to the rolling hills yonder she saw the mist come down, sweeping gracefully over the landscape like the train of an oyster satin wedding dress. The atmosphere of wonder and mystery it created reminded her of the huge adventure that was life. Anything could happen at any time; that was the miracle. Life was spontaneous, no matter how you tried to control it, and even if you didn't have a clue as to how things would unfold you just couldn't fail to be struck by the magic and symmetry of it. Out of something bad…good had come. She just had to be awed by that.

'What are you doing out here all on your own?'

Recently showered, Evan came up behind her, encircling her waist with his arms and urging her back to lean against him. Needing no coercion whatsoever, Rowan smiled and leaned into his quiet, implacable strength as if she'd been doing it for years. Immediately her senses were swamped by him, her heart increasing its rhythm just because he had touched her.

'Hmm…you smell nice.'

Shutting her eyes, she breathed him in, secretly

thrilled at the fact that since they'd been home he'd hardly been able to keep his hands off her. Now again she experienced the stirrings of desire, feeling wanton and wild and—for once in her life—totally carefree. It must be the influence of the weather, she thought. Misty and mysterious, it called to something elemental in her soul.

'You smell nice too.' He sniffed appreciatively. 'Like summer.'

'I was waiting for you,' she told him softly, her voice threaded with love.

'And I think I've been waiting for you for the whole of my life.' Nuzzling her neck, Evan moved his hands up to the soft swell of her breasts beneath her cardigan and cupped them. When he heard Rowan's sharp intake of breath, he undid the two small rose-pink buttons that fastened it, then circled her nipples with his thumbs beneath the thin gossamer material of her dress. Immediately he felt them bead, and was instantly aroused by the revelation that she wasn't wearing a bra.

'You're a wicked woman, Rowan Hawkins. You've turned into a little temptress right under my nose.' Warming to his plan to seduce her right here in the garden, with the dewy grass beneath her back, Evan slid his hands up the outsides of her thighs beneath the floaty dress and started to ease down her silky underwear.

'You mean I wasn't before?' Her voice teasing and husky, Rowan gasped a little as she obligingly stepped out of her panties, then thrilled to feel Evan's arousal press provocatively against her as he urged her back against him. Feeling herself dampen as her excitement grew, she slid her hand over his as he cupped her breast again—feverish now with longing and the greedy demand of need. It had come as a complete surprise to her that being pregnant seemed to make her exquisitely sensitive, and Evan's clever, tactile fingers seemed to know just where to touch her to drive her wild.

'You always knew how to tempt me, sweetheart. I swear you must have put some kind of love drug in those delicious pies of yours. But it's not food I want now.'

'Then what do…you want?' Her breath escaped on a rasp as he slid his hands from her breasts to her waist before dipping them down between her thighs and inserting his fingers into her dampness. 'Oh, God…Evan.'

'This is what I want,' he said hoarsely, his mouth on the side of her neck. 'You. All of you. I want to satiate myself in your heat and your sweetness and then do it all over again because I just can't seem to get enough of you.'

His craving for her growing more and more urgent as his fingers dipped in and out of the hot, sweet moistness between her silken thighs, Evan clasped her to him as she cried out and sagged against him. Then, giving her no time to recover, he urged her down onto the lush, damp grass, unzipped his jeans and plunged inside her, the relief and pleasure of possession drowning him in eroticism and the wild, untrammelled nature of their coupling.

Moments later, when he'd spilled his seed deeply

and hotly inside her, Evan drew Rowan tenderly into his arms and kissed her as if he never wanted to stop. Freeing her lips and pushing at his chest to make him pause for a moment, she laughed up into his protesting green eyes, stunned by the love and the need she saw there in the darkened pupils, wondering if it was possible to love somebody too much. Because what she felt for this amazing, gorgeous, sexy man seemed to go beyond merely being in love.

'What is it?' he growled now, impatient to taste her sweet lips again. 'Why did you make me stop?'

'I was wondering if we were going to have a boy or a girl. Do you have a preference?'

'Boy or girl, I'm going to love them to bits.'

A burst of warmth filled Rowan's chest with delight. 'So...you always wanted children, then?'

For a fleeting moment the laughter went out of his slumberous green gaze to be replaced by a drifting shadow. 'When I thought Rebecca was carrying my child—even though the marriage wasn't all it should have been—I thought it was the most wonderful thing that had ever happened. Then, when I found out she'd lied and the baby wasn't mine...I felt somehow bereaved. As if something precious had been stolen from me. I carried that emptiness around with me for a long time when she left to go and live with my friend. That was partly why I was so bitter and twisted about her betrayal. So the answer to your question, sweetheart, is yes...I *always* wanted children.'

'So we're going to have more than one, then?'

Dimpling, Rowan gazed up at him with teasing brown eyes.

Rescuing a blade of grass out of her hair, Evan threw it to one side, then slid his hands possessively onto her breasts. Feeling her heartbeat quicken, he smiled a smile that would melt an ice floe. 'Two or three at least. But first I think we need to get some much-needed practice in, don't you?'

'If this is practice, I can't wait to see what it will be like when you become expert.'

'Witch!'

'Lover…hmm.' Tightening her arms around his neck, Rowan pulled him down to offer her lips, all thoughts of past hurts and remembered pain banished for now at least, safe in the knowledge that her and her baby's future were inextricably linked with the most wonderful man in the world.

'I was longing for the summer,' she whispered just before her lips met his, 'and now it's here at last.'

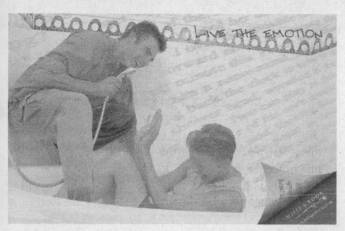

4 FREE

books and a surprise gift!

We would like to take this opportunity to thank you for reading this Mills & Boon® book by offering you the chance to take FOUR more specially selected titles from the Modern Romance™ series absolutely FREE! We're also making this offer to introduce you to the benefits of the Reader Service™—

- ★ FREE home delivery
- ★ FREE gifts and competitions
- ★ FREE monthly Newsletter
- ★ Exclusive Reader Service offers
- ★ Books available before they're in the shops

Accepting these FREE books and gift places you under no obligation to buy, you may cancel at any time, even after receiving your free shipment. Simply complete your details below and return the entire page to the address below. *You don't even need a stamp!*

YES! Please send me 4 free Modern Romance books and a surprise gift. I understand that unless you hear from me, I will receive 6 superb new titles every month for just £2.69 each, postage and packing free. I am under no obligation to purchase any books and may cancel my subscription at any time. The free books and gift will be mine to keep in any case.

P4ZED

Ms/Mrs/Miss/Mr ....Initials.................................
                                                      BLOCK CAPITALS PLEASE
Surname ....

Address ....

....

....Postcode..............................

Send this whole page to:
UK: FREEPOST CN81, Croydon, CR9 3WZ
EIRE: PO Box 4546, Kilcock, County Kildare (stamp required)

Offer valid in UK and Eire only and not available to current Reader Service subscribers to this series. We reserve the right to refuse an application and applicants must be aged 18 years or over. Only one application per household. Terms and prices subject to change without notice. Offer expires 31st October 2004. As a result of this application, you may receive offers from Harlequin Mills & Boon and other carefully selected companies. If you would prefer not to share in this opportunity please write to The Data Manager, PO Box 676, Richmond, TW9 1WU.

Mills & Boon® is a registered trademark owned by Harlequin Mills & Boon Limited.
Modern Romance™ is being used as a trademark.
The Reader Service™ is being used as a trademark.